JUSTICE REGAINED

By

G. Lee Greer

This book is a work of fiction. Places, events, and situations in this story are purely fictional. Any resemblance to actual persons, living or dead, is coincidental.

© 2003 by G. Lee Greer. All rights reserved.

No part of this book may be reproduced, stored in a retrieval system, or transmitted by any means, electronic, mechanical, photocopying, recording, or otherwise, without written permission from the author.

ISBN: 1-4107-7999-8 (e-book)
ISBN: 1-4107-7998-X (Paperback)
ISBN: 1-4107-7997-1 (Dust Jacket)

Library of Congress Control Number: 2003095501

This book is printed on acid free paper.

Printed in the United States of America
Bloomington, IN

1stBooks – rev. 08/01/03

Dedication

In loving memory of my mother, Gertrude Frances Vaughn Greer. A remarkable lady who made a lot of sacrifices for me.

Acknowledgements

Special thanks to my friend, Adolph Galindo, who shared his extensive knowledge of weapons with me, to Miriam Campbell, whose knowledge of computers saved me on many occasions, and to my wife, Betty, for her support and encouragement.

"In the world men must be dealt with according to what they are and not what they ought to be."

      Charles C. F. Greville

"There are those who, with deliberate perversity, demand their rights so as to violate the rights of others, who invoke the constitution only to tread on the constitution, who pretend to take refuge in freedom only to end all freedoms."

      Gustavo Diaz Ordaz
       Former President
      Republic of Mexico

JUSTICE REGAINED

Chapter 1

Boone "Peck" Reynolds was clearly agitated with himself. As he paced the floor of his office on the top floor of the Reynolds-Commerce building he muttered to himself about his indecision; It's time to fish or cut bait. You've thought this thing through inside out, upside down, and over and under. You have struggled with and agonized over the morality of it. Now, it is either move forward or forget it forever. What is it going to be, Peck? Your whole life has been built on making tough decisions. Granted, this is your toughest but it requires an answer now. Now!

The Reynolds-Commerce building was located in the heart of the financial district of Manhattan. It was late Friday afternoon and everyone was bailing out of the city, scattering in all directions, seeking a short reprieve from the hectic, maddening pace of the week just ended, before returning Monday morning to relive it all again.

Reynolds-Commerce had begun over five decades earlier as Reynolds Family Bank in Beaufort, South Carolina. Family Bank, founded by Peck's father, Boone Sr., began as a checking and savings bank as the country was working its way through the depression. He had slowly built his bank and his reputation by personal attention to his customer's needs and desires, as long as those goals made financial sense. The list of clients who had gotten their start with loans and counsel from the old man was impressive, not only for the number but the notable names of success stories that had made their mark in the world and they never forgot him nor failed to acknowledge his essential contribution to their lives.

Now there was Reynolds-Commerce, a much different institution, run by Peck after his father passed away nearly thirty five years ago. Returning from Europe at the end of World War II as a major in the tank corps, Peck was installed as a teller in his father's bank. This was a big step down but as his father had declared, "An essential step in learning the business." When Boone, Sr. passed away, Peck acted on an idea he had been toying with for years to establish a private bank for the well heeled that would offer a myriad of financial services beyond checking and savings accounts and loans. He discussed his idea with his mother, a younger brother, and an older sister, all of whom were equal owners of the bank and they agreed even though it was a real roll of the dice for had it failed they would all lose everything. Thus was established Reynolds-Commerce in New York City, a subsidiary of Reynolds Family Bank.

The premise for Reynolds Commerce was simple. The minimum entry was an account balance of twenty five thousand dollars. The bank would buy or sell, at the customers' direction, stocks, bonds, foreign currencies, options, real estate, or any other hard asset the customer desired in both the domestic and foreign markets. The customer had to cover the losses on the spot to maintain the twenty five thousand dollar minimum. The customer also had the option to purchase one share of Reynolds-Commerce stock within one year at a price of one thousand dollars. After the first year the price for the option to that share of stock was established on the first working day of the New Year and was exercisable within twelve months. The initial share of stock was now worth a half million dollars and the minimum entry level was now one million dollars.

Peck Reynolds quietly and quickly built Commerce into a giant financial house known and respected world wide. He sat on numerous corporate boards and was heavily involved in civic affairs and philanthropic organizations. He was also a counselor to Presidents and had served one stint as Treasury Secretary. He had declined further service at the national level but he kept closely involved, behind the scene, in the political affairs of the nation.

Peck broke out of his reverie and moved across the room to his desk and the phone. He punched in intercom one and was quickly answered.

"Vincent, is there anyone left but you and me?" asked Peck.

"No, sir."

"Do you have any big plans for the weekend?"

"No, sir."

"Well, let's go down to the farm. Call the field and have Gil get the plane ready and then call down to the farm and tell them we'll be coming. I have a couple of calls to make but I should be ready to go in about fifteen minutes," advised Peck.

"Yes, sir," acknowledged Vincent.

Peck unlocked the desk drawer and pulled out another phone. It was not just any other phone but one specially encrypted so that only his and three other like phones could communicate. He punched in his password and speed dial one and waited. After four rings, the phone was answered.

"Yes."

"I think it is time to put our plan in motion," said Peck.

"I'm ready. Have you spoken to the other party?"

"Not yet. I wanted to clear with you first and if you're okay, I will make the call and, as we agreed, if there is unanimous consent we will proceed. If you don't hear from me by the end of the day you will know we are on go. If there is a problem, I will get back to you," said Peck. He disconnected and punched in speed dial two.

"Hello."

"The other party and I agree that it is time to proceed. We need your approval."

"We can't get started soon enough to suit me. Did you see the headlines this morning?"

"Yeah, it got my blood boiling too. I will keep you posted." he said and signed off.

Peck made his way to the private elevator where Vincent was waiting and they made their way down to the garage. On their way to the air field Peck engaged Vincent in conversation.

"Did you read the headlines this morning, Vincent?"

"Yes sir and I still can't believe it. How can you ignore a dead body with three rounds in the head?"

The headline had read, JUDGE THROWS OUT DEAD BODY AS EVIDENCE.

"Pretty incredible, isn't it?"

"You would think that the important thing would be to bring the scumbag who killed the man to justice. This country is being led down the road to collapse by people like this judge. They are trying to build a perfect world by judicial decree, completely ignoring man's human nature, and we are letting them get by with it to our own self destruction," Vincent passionately offered.

"What do you think we can do about it at this stage?" inquired Peck.

"I don't know, Mr. Reynolds, but someone had better damn well do something or this country is going to see anarchy and that's not a pleasant thought either." said Vincent.

The remainder of the trip to the airfield was taken in silence and when they arrived Gil had the plane revved up and ready to go. The flight down to the landing strip near the farm was only forty five minutes and upon arrival Mr. Briggs, the caretaker, was waiting with the car and they made their way to the farm.

The farm was a three hundred acre spread in the rolling hills of Virginia horse country, about a forty five minute drive from downtown D.C. Peck didn't have the farm worked but he allowed a couple of good neighbors to use the pastures and plant hay and store horses in the horse barn. In turn, they looked after things and kept things in good order.

After an early dinner and a brandy with Vincent, Peck decided to call it a day. He said to Vincent, "I will see you for breakfast around eight and after we'll walk around the place. I have something I want to talk with you about."

"Goodnight, sir. I'll see you at breakfast."

The next morning after breakfast they strolled around the pastures and through the barns, admiring the quiet and beauty of the property. The horses being stabled there were pure thoroughbreds and Peck thought to himself that maybe he should raise some of his own horses but he quickly discounted that. He had the advantage of admiring the animals from afar without the concerns and hassle that ownership brings.

"Let's go in to the den and have another cup of coffee and we'll talk," said Peck.

As they sat quietly sipping their coffee Peck sensed that Vincent was curious about what they would be talking about and he opened the conversation with, "How long have you been with me, Vincent?"

"Well, sir, I guess that would be all my life."

"No, I mean as my full time assistant."

"Well then, that would be when I finished Columbia Law and came to Commerce. I wasn't your full time assistant then though. You had me doing a lot of things for awhile before I became your full time assistant, so I guess that would be about ten years ago," Vincent offered.

Peck recalled when Vincent was born and before that when he first met Vincent's mother and father. It was May 1945 and he was a tank company commander serving in Patton's fabled Third Army in Europe. The war was winding down; the Russians were beating on the door of

JUSTICE REGAINED

Berlin and it was just a matter of days before it would all end.

Peck had been ordered to skirt around Berlin and drive into Czechoslovakia: Patton had been ordered to avoid entering Berlin before the Russians, so he obeyed the orders literally, though he didn't like them, and avoided Berlin, but drove further east to establish a presence just in case Eisenhower came to his senses and allowed further advance into Eastern Europe. Peck's company made record speed and rolled into the town square of a small town in central Czechoslovakia where he came upon a young man and girl being held by Russian soldiers and the man being severely beaten by what appeared to be a Russian major.

Peck jumped from his jeep and yelled, "Let those people go."

The major looked up at the young American major and then went right back to beating the young man. Peck advanced quickly, pulling his 45 from the holster and jacking a round into the chamber and screaming even louder, "Let them go now or I will kill you where you stand."

As the major slowly turned to face this brash young American officer his men leveled their weapons on Peck and with that came a similar response from Peck's men, including the whirring of turrets and the ratcheting of rounds into the machine guns. The Russian major, realizing that he was seriously outgunned, tried another tack and said, "I am Major Nicholi Barshefsky and I am in charge of this sector, which is under Russian control. You will leave immediately heading west and I will forget your impertinence."

"It has yet to be determined as to who is in charge of what and I am not going anywhere and I will repeat it just one more time; let the man and woman go," Peck said and hoped that he was right but he had no idea what, if anything had been decided concerning occupation.

"What is your name, major?" inquired the Russian.

"I am Major Reynolds."

"Major Reynolds, these two are not worth an incident between two great allies; they have just been married and I was offering my services, as the ranking member in this sector, to break in the bride for the young man as is the old custom in my country. The young man took exception to my offer so I had to teach him proper respect for authority."

"Well, I would think that he has learned his lesson so if you would be so kind as to let them go now we can avoid an incident between two great allies, as you said."

The Russian major stared into the determined eyes of this young American major and said, "Release them." When the Russians let them go, the young man and woman rushed to the American major and stood frightened behind him.

"Thank you, major," Peck said. My company will be camped just to the west of town. I'll talk to you again before we pull out, if we pull out."

"Please take us with you, blurted out the young man in broken English. We cannot stay here. He will kill us."

"Lieutenant, take this young couple back to our command post. We will try to let the situation calm down and help them if we can. We are certainly not going to let our Russian friend get his hands on them again," directed Peck.

After the young couple was led away, Peck conversed with the Russian major and they worked out a suitable arrangement so that they would not step on each others toes until orders were given to one or the other or both. Upon returning to the command post he queried the lieutenant as to what, if anything, he had learned of the young couple.

"Their names are Georgi and Anna Havel. They were married this morning but they are not from this town. They were trying to make their way to Prague where the young man hoped to find work with an uncle who had promised him a job. They are scared to death, major. I hope we can find some way to help them."

"We'll see. Bring them in. I want to talk with them," ordered Peck.

The lieutenant returned in a matter of minutes with the young couple in hand. Though they were a little more relaxed Peck could see that they were still very fearful and apprehensive.

"My lieutenant says that you are trying to get to Prague. Are you aware that the Russians are in control of all territory east of here and that if you attempt to travel east you are probably going to run into a lot more Russians like the major?" asked Peck.

"Take us with you, please," pleaded the young man.

"Unfortunately we are still fighting a war and I can't take you with us other than to a more westerly position where the Russians haven't advanced," answered Peck.

"We go to America with you," said the young woman.

Peck smiled and said, "Lieutenant, feed these people and issue them blankets. We will take them with us when we return to headquarters and turn them over to the civil affairs people."

"Yes sir," said the grinning lieutenant.

As it turned out Peck was able to do more than just help them. When ordered to pull back, he had taken them with him and when they had reached headquarters he was able to pull a few strings, call in a few favors, and put in motion a plan to get them to America.

After arranging passage for the Havels, Peck cabled his father in Beaufort and asked him to meet the Havels in New York and get them to Beaufort. He would write in greater detail later but he knew that his father would be in New York to meet them.

Thus Georgi and Anna Havel came to America and took up residence in Beaufort, South Carolina, living in a guest house behind the main house. Georgi tended the grounds at home and performed odd jobs at the bank. Anna became the housekeeper and they were happy and flourished, producing Vincent within a year of arrival, and later a sister named Olga, and another son named Henri.

Boone, Sr. had seen to their education. After graduating from the University of South Carolina, Vincent took a commission in the navy for a three year stint to fulfill an ROTC obligation and afterward had taken his law degree at Columbia University while living with and working part time for Peck. Olga, his sister had become an accomplished pianist and had married well and Henri, the younger brother, worked for the family at the Beaufort bank. Georgi and Anna never tired of telling the story of how the dashing young major had rescued them and brought them to America. The children had heard the story a thousand times but they always grinned and bore it another time to please their parents. The family's allegiance to the Reynolds was deep and strong.

Georgi and Anna had moved into the main house at Peck's request, after his father's death, to look after his mother, who was now eighty-five years of age. He remembered that he must call his mother this weekend as he did every week. He knew that his mother worried about him, as mothers do, regardless of the age of the children, and he knew she worried even more since his wife passed away.

"Vincent, what I am about to discuss with you is extremely sensitive and highly confidential and what I am going to propose to involve you in is illegal. You are under no obligation to involve yourself and if you elect not to do so it will not affect our relationship whatsoever. If you say no, all that I ask is that you forget that the conversation ever took place."

"That goes without saying, sir."

"Good enough. Vincent, do you recall the conversation we had yesterday about that judge's decision and your comment that someone had damn well better do something about it?" asked Peck.

"Yes, sir."

"Well, a couple of others and I are going to do something about it. We are going to remove from our midst some of the most egregious members of our society, who violate the sensibilities of the vast majority of civilized people, and send a message to others who would use our institutions and laws to destroy this great country," said Peck. "I'm taking the lead on this and I need someone I can trust to make certain contacts and relay messages from time to time, so you would be intimately involved as a fellow conspirator, if you will, and if things go awry you would be vulnerable along with the rest of us. That being said, I will give you some time to think about it and you can let me know if you are in," said Peck.

"Sir, I don't need time to think about this. If I had the means and wherewithal to do it I would do it myself. I would be proud to be a part of this and I thank you for your confidence," said Vincent.

"You are absolutely sure?" asked Peck.

"Yes, sir. When do we get started?"

Peck removed a slip of paper from his pocket and handed it to Vincent. "We are going to stay over here a couple of extra days. On Monday morning, I want you to call this guy and set up a meeting with him for Tuesday afternoon. If he agrees, I want you to call the second name on the list and arrange to meet with him on Tuesday morning. The second guy on the list is a makeup artist and he will give you a different appearance. You will never have sight contact with the first guy again but I don't want him to be able to clearly identify you, just in case. Don't make the phone calls from here; find a pay phone and call from there. Memorize the information and destroy the paper. If everything goes as planned, here is what I want you to say to the first named man," instructed Peck.

On Monday morning Vincent made the phone calls as instructed and the meetings were agreed to. The makeup artist inquired as to what the gentlemen was looking for and Vincent replied that he needed a different appearance for temporary purposes and would discuss further at their appointment.

On Tuesday morning Vincent arrived at the makeup artist's address at ten AM. It was a nondescript, hole-in-the-wall space on the fringe of the business district of Washington, D.C. A bell tinkled as he entered the room and immediately a man came from the rear to meet him. "Good morning, sir. I assume that you are the gentleman who called yesterday."

"That is correct."

"I believe you said yesterday that you required a different look for a short period of time. Is that correct?"

"Yes, I'll leave it to you."

"If you will come with me, we'll get started."

They entered a back room and Vincent was directed to a barbershop style chair. The makeup man began immediately and by noon he handed Vincent a mirror for his appraisal. Vincent could not believe that he was looking at himself. His face seemed to have a different shape; his eye color was different; and his hair had been restyled and dyed.

"You do good work. My own mother wouldn't know me," offered Vincent. "I believe that one thousand dollars was mentioned yesterday."

"That is correct, sir."

Vincent counted out twelve one hundred dollar bills and handed them to the man. "A tip for your excellent service," he said.

The man removed some bottles from the shelf and handed them to Vincent with the instructions, "Your new look will last up to forty eight hours, barring rain or baths.

These items will remove your look at will; just follow the instructions"

"Thanks again. Good day."

Vincent had a couple of hours to kill before his next appointment so he decided to grab some lunch and let the world see his new look. Vincent was a striking figure of a man. At six foot three inches and two hundred and ten pounds, which he maintained by working out a minimum of three time a week, he was use to admiring looks from the ladies but was unaffected by it. With his new look, including a new hair style, blue eyes and a salt and pepper sprinkling of color on his temples he was getting even more attention from the ladies. As he ate his lunch he noticed on more one than one occasions that when he looked up there were one or more ladies looking at him and smiling. He returned their smiles and was inwardly amused by the whole thing. After lunch he made his way to his next appointment near the center of town, arriving at the building a few minutes early.

Upon entering the office marked O'Neal Associates he was greeted by a pleasant lady and after advising her that he had a two o'clock appointment, she told him that she would tell Mr. O'Neal that he had arrived and that it should only be a few minutes before he would see him.

In just a few minutes Jack O'Neal came out into the front office and extending his hand said, "Hi, I'm Jack O'Neal. Won't you come in?"

Vincent followed him into a well appointed inner office and noted the autographed photographs of some of Washington's well known players and began to

JUSTICE REGAINED

wonder if this was the guy he should be talking to. Trusting his boss, he set aside his reservations and began the conversation.

"Mr. O'Neal, you don't know me and I prefer to keep it that way and since you came highly recommended I am going to assume that our conversation is not being recorded and is confidential," said Vincent.

Jack O'Neal smiled, pulled out the right top desk drawer and pressed a button, cutting off the tape recorder. "Now we can begin and for purposes of our conversation I'll just call you Mr. Smith, if that is all right, said O'Neal. And what service may I render for you?"

"That will be fine, Mr. O'Neal, and I will get right to the point. I am prepared to offer you a one million dollar retainer for your services. The money will be deposited in an off shore, numbered account of your choosing. For that retainer you will establish a team of no more that four operatives who will be engaged in the killing of certain targets which will be provided to you from time to time. For each target eliminated you will be paid an additional one half million dollars, the money being handled in the same way. From the money received you will be expected to cover all expenses including your associates. The targets will be well known, high profile persons who could be from anywhere in the country. At no time is there to be more than one operative engaged on a single target and they will not know of the existence of the other operatives. It would be preferable if the operatives were located in different parts of the country; maybe East, South, Midwest, and West Coast," said Vincent.

"I can see a problem already. If these deaths are to look accidental it may take two or more persons working together to pull it off," said O'Neal.

"That will not be a problem. I am not concerned that the deaths look like an accident. As a matter of fact, it would be preferable if they did not," stated Vincent.

Vincent continued, "You will have complete latitude as to who you use and how the job is performed and your payment will be made immediately upon confirmation of the job. If you agree to the arrangement, you will be provided with an encrypted phone which will be used to advise you of the targets and I assume that you will develop a similar arrangement with your team members. My incoming number will be blocked so you will have no way to contact me. The contact will always be from me to you. Questions so far?"

"I don't suppose you would be willing to share with me who recommended me or who you work for?"

"As to the first, I am not privy to that information. As to the second, no."

"Is there anything else you need to tell me before I make my decision?"

"Yes. Once you have determined your team members I will need their names and locations, just in case something happens to you."

"I'm not too keen on that idea but, I guess, under the circumstances, I can understand. What do you need from me other than my decision?"

"I'll need your preference as to the off shore account and an account number of at least eight digits."

"Mr. Smith, if you would, keep your seat or help yourself to a drink from the bar over there. Bear with me for a few minutes and I will give you a decision," O'Neal said as he excused himself from the room.

Jack O'Neal left the office and walked out of the building on to the street. He needed some fresh air to help him absorb this proposal out of the blue. His investigative and security business, along with some darker assignments, had been good for him since he had retired from the CIA as the assistant director for operations but this job was staggering in both the risk and the financial reward. As he walked around the block, he began to think not of whether he would accept the job but who he would use and how he would operate. By the time he returned to the entrance of his building he had made his decision.

He reentered his office with a nod and sat down at his desk. He wrote down the name of a bank in Grand Cayman and jotted down an eight digit number, handing it to Vincent with the words, "I accept your proposal, Mr. Smith."

"I will advise you when the account has been established and you will be able to call the bank to confirm," Vincent said as he removed the encrypted phone from his briefcase and handed it to O'Neal. "You can program it to ring, beep, or vibrate. If you receive a call and cannot talk just press the pound sign and try to make yourself available to receive another call within thirty minutes. For further security you will answer by saying; testing, one, two, three, four. The reply will be; test confirmed, after which you will say: and what may I do for you today? Always use those exact words," Vincent said.

Rising and shaking Vincent's hand, O'Neal said, "I will need about a week to set things up after which I will be in a position to accept your first assignment. I look forward to a most interesting and profitable enterprise."

"Goodbye, Mr. O'Neal."

Vincent was beginning to sweat by the time he pulled out of the parking lot of O'Neal's building but he was pleased with himself. Driving back to the farm, he decided to test out his disguise and upon arriving he pulled up to the front entrance of the house, got out of the car and rang the doorbell. The door was answered by Mrs. Briggs who had known Vincent for over ten years. Using his best Boston accent, Vincent stated that he would like to see Mr. Reynolds.

"Please wait here, sir, and whom shall I say is calling?" inquired Mrs. Briggs.

"Mr. Smith, madam."

Peck came to the door and introduced himself.

"It's me, sir, Vincent. I just wanted to see how you would react to my disguise"

"Well, I'll be damned. Come on in and fill me in."

"If you don't mind, sir, I would like to become myself again first. It shouldn't take but about thirty minutes. I will come straight down to the den."

Jack O'Neal was pensive as he reviewed the files of a number of personnel he knew and had used over the years. Since retiring from the CIA as assistant to the deputy director for operations his life had been pretty simple, comparatively speaking, to his years of active service at CIA. He had had occasions to be involved in some pretty

JUSTICE REGAINED

significant contracts since leaving the Agency, most of which had been farmed out to him by the Agency itself, but he knew that this mother of all contracts was overwhelmingly the most important and riskiest he would ever undertake. It would require the very best planning, personnel, and execution possible. He did not know the targets to be hit but he did know that they were not going to be nobodies whose demise would not register on the screen of public opinion.

He had already settled on three of the four people he wanted to use: Joe Rollins, ex navy seal, Don Casciolini, ex army ranger, and Angela Robechek, ex CIA and suspected mafia contractor. After reading and rereading the files of two finalists for the fourth slot, he settled on Pam Wallace, ex Chicago cop. He chuckled to himself that he was being politically correct in choosing two male and two female assassins.

He called Casciolini first and recognizing the voice that answered and without identifying himself said, "I'm going to be in Boston tomorrow and would like to meet with you to discuss some potential work you can do for me. I will be flying in and out with just two hours between flights, so why don't we meet in the conference room at the USAir Club at ten AM. I will reserve the space."

"I'll see you there."

Subsequent calls to the other three enabled him to lay out an itinerary of Boston, Chicago, Los Angeles, Atlanta, and back to Washington in just two days.

G. Lee Greer

Chapter 2

As Vincent told Peck of his meeting with Jack O'Neal, Peck was pleased to see everything falling into place. He knew of O'Neal's reputation and who had recommended him and was at ease with this first step.

"Vincent, you have the matching phone to O'Neal's so be sure you have it available when needed. I have to set things in motion to get the account set up in Grand Cayman. It should not take too long and when it's done, I want you to ring O'Neal and confirm that the account has been established. I am sure he will want to call the bank to verify. I have some calls to make so why don't you get hold of Gil and tell him we will fly back to New York in the morning," said Peck.

"Yes, sir."

After Vincent left the room, Peck pulled out his encrypted phone, punched in his password and speed dial one. The call was answered immediately.

"I am between meetings and this is the first free moment I have had all day. Your call was opportune."

"I just wanted you to know that the first phase has been completed successfully and we should be able to start in about ten days to two weeks. You need to think about your first candidate nomination. I will be doing the same and I will advise our friend likewise. I will be back in touch when we are ready to go," said Peck.

"I look forward to hearing from you." And with that, speed dial one punched out.

The call to speed dial two went the same and Peck then keyed in speed dial three, his money man who would handle the financial transfers. He was in Geneva and handled financial matters for Peck on a regular basis, completely trustworthy, and he had to be since he had access to and authority on Peck's Swiss accounts. He instructed his agent to set up the Grand Cayman account, giving him the account number O'Neal had provided.

"This should be completed in about fifteen minutes. Is there anything else, sir?"

"No, that is it for today. I will talk with you later."

Peck found Vincent and told him to call O'Neal and tell him he could confirm Grand Cayman at his convenience.

"The plane will be ready from seven o'clock on tomorrow morning," advised Vincent.

"Good. Let's get some dinner and we will tell Mrs. Briggs to plan on breakfast about seven."

Peck was back in his office at Commerce by ten the next morning when he received a phone call from his long time friend, Bob Peters.

"Peck, how are you?"

"I'm doing well, and you Bob?"

JUSTICE REGAINED

"Things couldn't be better. My doctor says I have the body of a forty year old, my wife still adores me for the charmer I am, and you're continuing to make money for me. What more could a fellow ask?"

"Nothing, I guess. Sounds like you've got the perfect life and I can't think of anyone more undeserving than you with all the shenanigans you have pulled over the years. I assume you called for some reason other than to extol your virtues."

"Now, be kind, Peck. You know that I only speak the truth, but you are right, I do have an ulterior motive. The President is coming to town on Friday and he wanted me to get you and some of the other fellows together for a brief session."

"A session about what?"

"He didn't say but I suspect that he wants to get an early start on his fundraising for next year's reelection campaign and he is going to suggest some goals for each of us."

"What time and where?"

"Well, he is scheduled for an advertised, non-partisan affair celebrating an anniversary of the establishment of the United Nations at the UN at two o'clock and he would like to meet with us at the Waldorf around four. I have reserved a suite and it has been cleared by the Secret Service. I will see you there shortly before four, and thanks, friend."

"See you there, Bob, and it's good to talk with you."

Peck's secretary came into his office with the admonition, "Don't forget, you have the museum trustees meeting at the museum at seven. The driver will be out front at six forty five."

"Thanks, Helen, for reminding me, although I am not looking forward to mixing and mingling with most of them, a damn bunch of knee jerk liberals who are going to tell us what is wrong with this country. By the way, Bob Peters called and I am scheduled to meet with the President on Friday at four o'clock at the Waldorf and unless you have me obligated, I am going to scoot down to Beaufort for the weekend. Check with Vincent and see if he wants to go and have Gil revved up and ready to go by six. If Vincent is going I will ride out to the strip with him, otherwise schedule me a driver. And call Mom and tell her to look for us around eight. No need to call anyone else down there; Mom will spread the word."

"Yes sir."

"And thanks, Helen, for all you do to help keep me from going bonkers"

"You're welcome, boss."

Peck arrived a few minutes early for the museum trustee meeting and found the gathering in small clusters socially engaged in light, meaningless chatter. After greetings all around he was drawn to a conversation in which the speaker was offering his opinion of the courageous judge's ruling that had made headlines a few days ago.

"He was absolutely right to rule as he did. A busted tail light and the absence of a license plate is not probable cause for searching the driver's trunk. Those were misdemeanor offenses. He should have been issued a citation and sent on his way," offered the concerned speaker.

"What about the cop's statement that he was acting nervous and suspicious?" asked another member of the group.

"You would have been nervous too if you were black and had been stopped by two white cops."

Peck interjected, "Does the fact that a dead body was found in the trunk and that there is good reason to believe that the driver either killed the man or certainly knew something about the killing mean anything at all? Isn't the poor guy who was murdered and his family entitled to justice by holding the killer accountable?"

"The rights of the accused must be protected before all else and particularly for the underprivileged," opined the defender of the oppressed.

"Is there any place for common sense to come into play in the process without some misguided, guilt laden federal judge denying justice to the rest of society by letting this fellow take a walk and return to the street to kill someone else?" asked Peck.

"We must always safeguard the rights of the accused above all else and requiring the Gestapo style police to follow strict rules of procedures is little to ask," the speaker said.

Peck walked away from the group shaking his head as the meeting was being called to order.

G. Lee Greer

Chapter 3

Jack O'Neal was sipping coffee in a small conference room at the US Air club at Logan International, when with a quiet knock on the door, a club attendant announced the arrival of Mr. O'Neal's guest. When the door was closed, Don Casciolini said, "Hello, Jack."

"Good to see you, Don. I believe it's been almost two years seen I have seen you. You are looking as trim and fit as ever," Jack replied.

"Well, I try to stay in shape. In this crazy world you never know when or what you may be asked to do and to keep the bill collectors away from the door, you must be prepared to pick up a few dollars when you can."

Jack knew that a few dollars was the least of Don's worries. He had provided for himself very nicely, and if he never picked up another dollar, he wouldn't know the difference. In his early forties, ex-army ranger, having left the service after twelve adventuresome years in which he had built a solid reputation as an incredibly tough and bright leader, he had quickly established himself as one of the best in corporate and private security. One of his clients was a high rolling financier and Don had made a fortune in investing in ventures just from eavesdropping on conversations between his boss and partners or clients.

Don had left the service because he had become bored. At the time there was not a good war going on anywhere and there were no dark assignments to be had. The world had just gotten too soft so Don decided it was time for him to make some money. And he needed the money. After leaving the service Don had gotten married, and being the good catholic that he was, he was the father of five children.

"Don, I'll cut right to the chase. From time to time I am going to need the services of someone with your talents to take out a person or persons unknown at this time, but who I do know will be a high profile citizen. Their demise will not go unnoticed so it would be expected that there will be some heat applied. You would be entirely on your own with no backup or legal assistance to depend on. Because of the nature of the work, I will insist that you involve no one else in the project. It will not be necessary that the job be staged to look accidental; I believe the people who are engaging us are trying to send a message. That is just a guess at this point, but it's what I read into the situation," said Jack.

"It sounds interesting. Would there be any strict time frame requirement?" asked Casciolini.

"No, you would work on your own timetable, within reason, of course."

"And what kind of compensation are we talking about?"

"One quarter million dollars per contract, paid upon completion."

"That is per person, right?"

"Right."

"And how will it be paid?"

"Your call, but probably in cash by courier or, if you prefer, an off shore account."

"How will we communicate?" asked Don.

"There will be no communication except from me to you. I will set up a secure phone for you to receive and you will be given a name, address, and a brief bio so that there is no misunderstanding as to the target," advised Jack.

Don sat quietly for a couple of minutes and then said,

"Okay, I'm in."

Rising, Jack said, "Don, I look forward to doing business with you. I'm going to have to run. I have a plane to catch. It has been great seeing you. I will be in touch."

Thirty minutes later Jack was on his way to Chicago and his meeting with Pam Wallace. She met him at the gate and he suggested that since he would be overnighting in Chicago, they hold their conversation in the hotel room he had reserved. Pam drove Jack to the hotel and after checking in, they made their way to the room.

Pam Wallace was an enigma. A beautiful woman, about five foot two and one hundred fifteen pounds, she had that All-American cuddly look that stopped men in their tracks, but Jack knew better. She was as described but a whole lot more: tough as nails, skilled in weapons and martial arts, and not someone you would want to try to mug on a dark street. In her mid thirties, she was a college graduate and a ten year veteran of the Chicago police. She would still be there but there had been a little trouble with her method of extracting a confession from a child rapist which had resulted in the accused being set free. It had been quietly suggested that if she resigned it would be in her and the department's best interest. Her father and an uncle, both retired from the force, and a brother who was an active duty captain on the force, wanted her to stay and fight, but they all knew that even if she could hold onto her job, she was not going any higher than she was. Pam decided that she did not want the hassle, so she quietly resigned.

    She had had no trouble finding plenty to do for a lot more money, providing private bodyguard and consultant services in the Chicago area. She had worked for Jack on one prior occasion and she recalled that assignment. He had called her, introduced himself, and asked if she were interested in a short assignment right there in Chicago. He explained that he had a client whose daughter was being harassed by a gentleman who would not take no for an answer, and he would be very grateful if a message could be delivered in such a way as to make this guy go away. The job would pay ten thousand dollars, and she figured if she did it right the first time, it would take about half a day. She accepted.

    The gentleman lived in Evanston, just outside Chicago. Pam was able to get him on the phone and asked to make an appointment to meet with him either at home or at his office in the city. He inquired as to the nature of the meeting, but Pam, in her most sultry voice, told him she could not talk about it on the phone and suggested to him that it would very much be to his advantage to meet with her. Pam arrived at the gentleman's office the next day at the appointed time and, with one look, the gentleman was delighted that he had agreed to meet with her.

He invited her to sit on the small sofa in his office and he took a seat next to her. Pam immediately rose from her seat and pulled up a chair directly in front of him so close that their knees were touching. She took both his hands in hers and looking him straight in the eye said, "Sir, I have been asked to speak with you about your continued rude behavior towards one Samantha Collins. She does not desire your attention and if you persist any further I will visit upon you a beating that you cannot imagine. When I am through with you, your parents won't recognize you and I guarantee that your recovery period and therapy will be long. Now, all you have to do to avoid all this unpleasantness is to cease and desist with any contact whatsoever with the lady in question."

"Who the hell do you think you are, bitch? I will have you arrested and I'll sue your cute little ass for more money than you ever dreamed of," he blurted.

With that, Pam applied the slightest of backward pressure to his two little fingers as he gasped in pain and astonishment.

Pam said, "Sir, what can I tell my client?" May I tell him that his daughter will not be hearing from you anymore?"

"Please, let go of my fingers." Pam released the pressure but when he tried to get up from the couch, she quickly clamped down hard on the trapezius muscle on his shoulder in a vice like grip and he writhed in a new kind of pain. "Please, no more," he cried.

"Sir, I must have an answer to give my client and if it is the wrong answer I will have to assure him that I will follow through in a different way until we finally reach an understanding. So, Sir, what's it going to be?"

Pam released the pressure and, still sitting knee to knee and nose to nose, she could see the fear in his eyes, and she knew he would be no further trouble.

"She will never hear from me again," he said.

"The right, and a very wise decision, sir. Good day, sir," she said and with that she strolled from his office.

"Pam, are you hungry?" asked Jack.

"I could eat a bite."

"Good. If it is all right with you, I will order up some room service so that we can talk privately. Why don't you look over the menu and we will get our order in." said Jack.

After the room service order was placed Jack opened the conversation with "Pam, I probably don't need to say this but I have to. I must have your word that what we discuss here, stays here, whether you decide to associate yourself or not," said Jack.

"That goes without saying."

"Good. Pam, I am not sure that this work is your cup of tea. To my knowledge you have never engaged in this kind of assignment but I would like for you to consider it. It involves the taking of life, assassination, if you will, and the targets will be a little higher up the social ladder than Joe Sixpack. The targets will be designated by the people who hired me and I will go ahead and tell you that I don't know who he, she, or they are. You will work entirely alone and have complete freedom as to how you do the job. Upon successful completion you will be paid one quarter million dollars. I don't know how many targets will be assigned to you. At this point, I can just say, one or more."

"You're right. I have never taken on this kind of work. Do you have any idea who these targets will be?"

"No, I don't, other than to say that I am sure that they won't be some little old lady who occasionally exceeds the posted speed limit."

"Would I have a choice as to whether I accept or reject a particular assignment once the target is revealed to me?"

"No. Unless there is some unusual circumstance. You are either in or out."

"When do you need my answer?" asked Pam.

"Unfortunately there is not much time. I am committed to having this set up pretty quickly. I will be flying out at ten in the morning and I will need your answer by then. I will be in my room here until around eight o'clock and you can give me a call. If I do not hear from you by then I will assume that you are not interested."

The room service dinner was delivered and they talked more as they ate.

"Jack, are these political assassinations?" asked Pam.

"Pam, until such time as the targets are named I do not know anything. I would only be guessing. Once the targets are revealed, both of us may know more about what this is about. My best guess at this point, and I stress the word guess, is that someone is trying to send a message to certain people or groups of people. That is all I can tell you," answered Jack.

"Will I be working with others?" asked Pam.

"No. You will be entirely on your own and I mean your own. If you get into trouble, you will have to handle it the best way you can. As far as this is concerned, I don't know you and you don't know me," replied Jack.

After discussing how payment and contact would be handled, Pam seemed satisfied that she had all the information she needed. She said good night and departed.

While having breakfast in his room the next morning, Jack's phone rang. He answered, "Yes."

"I'm on board. I will wait to hear from you."

Jack made his way to the airport for the flight to Los Angeles.

When Jack stepped outside the baggage claim in Los Angeles, he spotted Angela Robechek waiting for him. He threw his bags into the back seat and got into the car. "Let's go somewhere where we can talk privately. I have a flight back out to Atlanta at six. That should give us plenty of time," he said.

"I have a condo about twenty five minutes from here. That should be private enough."

After arriving at the condo, Angela asked, "May I fix you a sandwich or would you like to have a drink?"

"Thanks, but no on the sandwich. I ate on the plane, but even though it's only two o'clock here, my east coast body is telling me it's five, so I'll have a scotch rocks if you have it."

"Coming right up."

While sipping his drink, Jack went through the same spiel he had with Don and Pam. Angela's questions were almost identical. It did not take long for Angela to sign on. This was right up her alley.

Angela Robechek was an assassin by trade and she had been trained by the best. She was ex-CIA and Jack was very familiar with her work. She had retired from the CIA at the young age of forty one with twenty years service. For twelve of those years, before Jack had retired, she had worked for him. She did other things now but Jack knew that this was where her heart was and she was damn good at it. Maybe the best he had ever known. He was pleased to have her on his team.

"Jack, I would appreciate it if you could throw at least two assignments my way. I've got my eye on a little piece of property back in the hills where it would be just me and three or four horses. I could sure use the money for my dream home," said Angela.

"I will throw everything I can your way, Angela. I feel sure that there will be more than one, but I can't promise it. Let's see how it goes. And now we need to be heading back out to the airport," said Jack.

In Atlanta, Jack took a room at a hotel near the airport. The next morning he walked next door to a waffle house and, using a pay phone, called Joe Rollins, gave him the room number, and asked him to come over. After hanging up the phone and making his way back to his room, Jack thought about Joe and what he knew of him. A strapping six foot four, two hundred twenty five pound black guy with a shaved head, he was the personification of intimidation. He was ex-seal, having retired three years earlier. Despite his appearance Joe was soft spoken and reticent. You almost had to drag conversation out of him. If two words would convey the message, then Joe used only two words.

His service jacket revealed a dedicated and highly efficient operative. He had been involved in some very top secret missions and his superiors' reports had been glowing. He had received many commendations and medals though most of them could not be revealed because of the nature and location of his work. He had done one job for Jack since retiring and it had gone smoothly, without a hitch.

About an hour after calling him, Joe arrived. Jack ran through the proposal with Joe, trying to cover all the questions that the other three had asked. When he had finished, Joe said, "I'm in."

"Just like that. You don't have questions or need some time?" Jack asked.

"No."

"It's going to be a pleasure doing business with you, Joe."

Joe left and, shortly afterward, Jack was winging his way back to Washington. Things had gone better than expected. He had the four people he wanted most and would not have to go to his backup list. It had been a good two days work.

Two weeks later, Peck called Vincent into his office and said, "It has been two weeks since you talked with our man and I believe he said he would need a week or two to set things up. Give him a call and see if he is ready to proceed."

"Yes, sir, I'll do that right now."

JUSTICE REGAINED

Vincent returned to his office and removed his special phone from the locked drawer and keyed in speed dial one. The answer came almost immediately: "Testing, one, two, three, four."

"Test confirmed."

"And what may I do for you today?"

"I just need to know if you are ready to proceed."

"Yes."

"Good, I will be in touch soon."

Vincent returned to Peck's office and advised him that everything was ready.

"Good. I need to make some calls. I will get back to you later."

When Vincent left the office, Peck took out his special phone and keyed in speed dial one. There came back an immediate buzz which told Peck that the call had been received, and that the party could not talk right then, but would be ready to take his call in thirty minutes.

Thirty minutes later, he called again and was answered by, "I was tied up but I am clear now for a few minutes."

"Everything is set up and ready to go and we need to settle on our first candidate," said Peck.

"Do you have anyone in particular in mind?"

"My thoughts are the judge in upstate New York who threw out the dead body as evidence," replied Peck.

"That sounds like a good beginning. You have my concurrence."

"Understood."

Peck signed off and keyed in speed dial two and the answer came almost immediately.

"We are ready to go. The other party and I agree that our first candidate should be the judge in upstate New York who threw out the dead body as evidence recently. We will need your concurrence or another recommendation," said Peck.

"Great minds think alike. I could not agree more."

"We will talk later."

Peck buzzed Vincent and asked him to step into his office. When Vincent arrived, Peck advised, "We are ready to proceed with our first candidate. You can contact our man and turn him loose. The candidate is federal district judge, Josiah Hammond, who, on appeal, threw out the dead body as evidence. Here are the particulars on this gentleman and remember, as soon as you have relayed the information, destroy the paper."

"Damn, I knew it. What a great choice. I will get right on it," said Vincent and, with that, he left the office.

Vincent keyed in speed dial one and after the proper response came, said, "I have your first assignment. He is federal district judge, Josiah Hammond, of Buffalo, New York. He lives at 3041 Mulberry, and he also has a fishing cottage somewhere on the south shore of Lake Erie."

"Holy shit, you people aren't fooling around, are you?"

"Do you have a problem?"

"No. I will get right on it."

Chapter 4

After the meeting with the President and Bob Peters, which was about fund raising for the President's re-election campaign, Vincent was waiting with the car outside the Waldorf. They drove to the airstrip for the flight down to Beaufort. On arrival, Peck's brother Bill was waiting with the car.
"Good to see you, Peck. Vincent"
"You too, Bill. I hope mother isn't going to make too big a deal out of this visit, Vincent and I just needed to get away for awhile to remind us how you people live the good life."
"Just family tonight but tomorrow half of Beaufort will be calling. Just close friends, mother said."
When they arrived at the Reynolds home, all of the family, including Vincent's, were waiting on the front porch. As they bounded up the stairs Mother Reynolds was waiting with outstretched arms to embrace Peck and then Vincent. After hugs all around they all went inside for a little libation and free flowing conversation before dinner, everyone catching up on things since they had all been together.

After dinner, Peck insisted that his mother retire with the assurance that they had all weekend to enjoy each others company. Shortly afterwards the others bid their goodnights and Peck and Vincent turned in early.

Peck lay in bed and thought about all the good times he had growing up in Beaufort, South Carolina. Beaufort, known as the "Queen of the Carolina Sea Islands, lying in the southeastern corner of the state along the Atlantic coast on the inland waterway, was rich in history and tradition.

Since it was discovered by the Spanish in 1514 and after two hundred years of feuding among the Spanish, French, English, and Scots, along with the Tuscarora and Yemassee Indians, who were trying to hold onto their claims to the land, the territory was finally chartered by the English in 1711.

It is the second oldest town in South Carolina and during the eighteenth century it thrived on indigo, rice and Sea Island cotton plantations. The 1980 census showed a countywide population of 63,364 and the town population of 8,634 but when Peck was growing up in the 20's and 30's the countywide population was less than 25,000 and the town population was 2,776 and everyone knew everyone else and looked out for each other.

Today, the ruins, historic forts and landmarks, elegant homes, Gullah culture and cuisine are a tapestry of Beaufort's rich, five hundred year history and it is dear to the hearts of Peck and his family whose ancestors are traced back in the area to the early eighteenth century.

Peck's thoughts shifted to his childhood sweetheart, Phyllis, whom he had married and lived with happily until her premature death with cancer. Shortly after they were married, they had moved to the New York area because of Peck's business but Peck knew, though she never said it, that his wife's heart was still in Beaufort and he regretted having torn her away from the life she loved. When the doctors told them of her terminal condition, Phyllis wanted to go home and Peck took her home to die, commuting back and forth, sometimes daily, so that he could spend as much time as possible with her. She lasted about five months but there were some good days when she thrived with her friends, family, and familiar surroundings. Peck and Phyllis had no children and they had lived totally for each other.

"Goodnight, my sweet Phyllis. I love you today as I did the first day, and I miss you so much," whispered Peck.

Vincent was restless too. He tried to sleep but it would not come. Seeing his family had made him realize how different his life was from what he had imagined it would be. He thought of his wife Teresa and his little boy, Eric, who had been killed by a drunk driver just three years after they had been married. Since their deaths, he had totally immersed himself in his life as Peck's right hand man and had shown no interest in getting into another relationship. Peck and Phyllis treated him like a son and they had tried to introduce him to suitable young ladies, as Phyllis called it, but he showed no interest. After Phyllis died it was just Peck and Vincent and they were devoted to each other. Peck had suggested that Vincent needed to get out on occasion, away from him and his work, and meet other people and do fun things.

Vincent had replied that he was probably right and that Peck should do the same. That closed the subject.

The next day was non stop. Bill had been right, Peck thought. At least half of Beaufort, friends of Peck and Vincent, dropped by to see them and they enjoyed seeing old friends and reminiscing about their earlier days. That night at dinner it was just family again plus Peck and Vincent's closet boyhood friends and the conversation was without pause. Mother Reynolds was glowing and Peck promised himself that he was going to come down more often to feed his soul and help to make his mother's last years as happy as possible.

"Peck, when are you going to shuck your life in the fast lane and come on back home?" asked Hank, Peck's closest boyhood friend.

"Hear, hear," chimed in Peck's sister, Sarah.

"Maybe sooner than you think. I'm getting too old for the New York and Washington lifestyle," replied Peck. He looked at his mother and saw a tiny tear inch its way down her cheek.

"And another thing. I have known you all my life but I still don't know why we call you Peck," said Hank.

Peck chuckled and said, "Well, it is certainly not because I look like Gregory Peck, but I will let my dear sister Sarah tell you, since she gave me the name."

"I thought everyone knew. He has been called Peck since he was six years old. It was the summer before Peck started school. Mother gave us peck buckets and sent us down the road to pick blackberries and told us to be back in two hours. Well, the vines were full and Peck ate his fill before he started filling his bucket. When we had our buckets full, we started back home and I decided that I wanted to take a dip in the creek. Peck didn't want to go in so he sat on the bank while I swam. When I came out of the water, there was Peck, lying on the ground, moaning and groaning, with his mouth and half his face as purple as could be. He had sat there and eaten a whole peck of blackberries on top of all he had eaten earlier. I had to literally drag him home and when we got there mother took one look at Peck and the empty blackberry bucket and asked, "Did you eat a whole peck of blackberries?"

"Peck just looked up at mother mournfully and promptly threw up all over the kitchen and for the next few days every time mother looked at him she would just shake her head and mutter; a whole peck. I started calling him Peck and every time I did he would grab a stick and try to whack me. The name stuck, though, and I believe that to this day, Peck still can't look a blackberry in the eye, much less, eat one," said Sarah.

As they all laughed, Peck said, "Regretfully, it is all true and by the time I started school everybody was calling me Peck and Sarah is right, to this day I don't want to be within a mile of any kind of blackberry."

Sunday, their last day, was spent peacefully in small talk and as they readied to depart Mother Boone pulled Peck aside and said, "Son, I'm worried about you. Please thoughtfully consider cutting back and coming home."

G. Lee Greer

"I will, mother. You will be seeing a lot more of me from now on. Every chance I get, I'll be home."

Chapter 5

Jack O'Neal called Don Casciolini and when answered said, "I have an assignment for you."

He gave him the name and pertinent data on the target and signed off.

Casciolini quickly threw together a travel bag, kissed his wife goodbye, and within one hour was traveling by car to Buffalo. His wife never asked questions. She had gotten use to his strange hours and quick trips, sometimes for days, but she trusted him and he was a good and devoted provider for his family. He had thought about flying but determined that he could move around easier without a paper trail if he used his own car. There would be no airport security or rental car agencies to deal with and no reason to have to identify himself to anyone.

He drove straight through to Buffalo and after securing a room in a small, nondescript motel just outside of the city, he had dinner at a nearby restaurant and turned in for the night. The next morning he made his way into the city and found the federal courthouse. He had some scout work to do. Inside the courthouse, he wandered around, taking note of the location of Judge Hammond's office, the court schedule and the fact that the honorable judge was presiding over a criminal trial. He made his way to the courtroom and quietly slipped into a seat on the back row to observe the judge in action.

Judge Josiah Hammond was in his element. He was presiding over the trial of a man charged with drug trafficking and firearms violations and the prosecution was laying out a rock solid case against the defendant. Armed with a properly executed search warrant, agents from the FBI, DEA, and ATF had raided the home of the accused and found ten kilos of crack cocaine, various other drugs in large amounts, without prescription, and numerous automatic weapons. It would seem that they had him cold and that upon conviction, he would have to serve a minimum of twenty five years.

The lead agent from the FBI was on the stand and after answering all the questions of the prosecution was being cross examined by the defense attorney.

"Agent Billows, when you entered the home of the defendant, exactly what did you do?"

"I advised the defendant that we had a search warrant for the premises and that he was to stand clear while we executed the search."

"Did you place the warrant in his hands?"

"Yes."

"And what did the defendant do?"

"He threw the warrant back at me."

"Agent Billows, are you saying that the defendant did not read the warrant?" asked the defense counsel.

"That's correct."

Judge Hammond interrupted. "Are you testifying, agent Billows, that the defendant did not read and understand the contents of the warrant?"

"As I testified, he threw the warrant back at me."

"And you felt no obligation to retrieve the warrant and read it to the defendant and make sure he understood what was going on?" continued the judge.

"Objection, your Honor, yelled the prosecutor as he jumped to his feet. The government is under no obligation to read the warrant to the defendant unless specifically requested to do so."

"Your Honor, interjected the defense attorney, it is clear to me and I am sure will be clear to the court that the search was conducted in an illegal and unconstitutional manner and I move that all the items seized during the search and all references thereto be suppressed."

The prosecutor could hardly contain himself. "Your honor, this is clearly not the law and there is no legal basis for consideration of this outrageous motion," he said.

"The law is what I say it is, Mr. Prosecutor, and I agree with the defense that the defendant was denied his constitutional rights and the introduction as evidence of any and all items seized during the raid is hereby suppressed."

The prosecutor fumed, "You cannot do that, your honor. There is absolutely nothing in the law to support it and I urge your reconsideration."

"I can and have done it, Mr. Prosecutor. I am a federal judge, elected for life. I can interpret the law as I see fit," retorted Judge Hammond.

"Exception, your Honor. The government requests a continuance of twenty four hours so that we may enter an emergency appeal to the district appellate court," pleaded the prosecutor.

"I will do better than that. You will have until Monday, 10:00 AM. That should give you plenty of time. Court is in recess," said the judge.

As the courtroom began to clear, Casciolini fell in behind the prosecution team as they exited the courtroom and as they stopped to talk he listened in on their conversation.

"All right, heads up guys. We are not about to let this liberal sonofabitch get away with this. It's Wednesday morning, so we have plenty of time, but I want to move on this immediately. We will assemble in the main conference room at one o'clock and draft our appeal. I overheard the judge tell the clerk that he was going fishing. Maybe we will get lucky and the asshole will fall out of his boat and drown," said the lead prosecutor.

Chapter 6

This is too easy, thought Casciolini. Going fishing meant just one thing to him, the judge's house on Lake Erie. He immediately made his way to his car and headed out in the general direction of the judge's retreat. A local map gave him good direction. He had the address, but he would need to find the specific location and scout out the place. He found the right cutoff from the main road and began cruising the area until he found the street, or more correctly the lane, on which the judge's house was located. It was an unpaved lane, more like a long driveway, and he slowly made his way down the lane to come to a single cabin directly on the water. It was the only house on the street. He did not leave the car but studied the area carefully, particularly looking for any close neighbors. There were none.

As he made his way back out to the main road he decided that he would head back toward Buffalo; he didn't want to be observed just sitting around and he figured that he needed to allow the judge plenty of time to make it out to his cabin. Nearing Buffalo he found a bar and grill and enjoyed a nice dinner. It was around eight o'clock as he made his way back up to the lake, but it was midsummer, so it was not yet completely dark. As he turned onto the judge's lane he cut his lights and slowly made his way down to the cabin and pulled off to the side when he spotted lights coming from the cabin.

He removed the silenced Glock from underneath the seat, exited the car and made his way to what was obviously the main entrance to the cabin. He knocked on the door and heard stirring within. Judge Josiah Hammond opened the door.

"Yes."

"Judge Hammond?"

"That's me."

Casciolini pulled the gun up from behind his leg and shot the judge through the heart. The judge crumpled to the floor and Casciolini pumped another round into the temple of the already dead Federal Judge Josiah Hammond.

Casciolini entered further into the cabin and turned off the coffee pot, which had been brewing, retrieved the brass shell casings, cut off all the lights and, after setting the latch to lock, he exited the cabin.

It was Saturday morning when the State police found the body. They had been requested by the judge's clerk to find the judge and have him call in. She had been trying to reach him since early Friday afternoon to tell him that the Court of Appeals had overturned his ruling in the drug case.

The State police found the judge's car at the cabin and after looking around and finding his boat still tied to the dock, they forced the door to the cabin and found the body.

Calls went out everywhere and the FBI assumed jurisdiction of the case since the victim had been a federal judge who was obviously murdered.

The place was swarming with federal people immediately, the site sealed off and the investigation begun. A week later they were no closer to solving this one. Literally, no one had seen or heard anything. The site was clean and they couldn't turn up a single clue to go on. They only knew that he had been shot twice, execution style, and other than the caliber of the weapon, they had nothing.

Jack O'Neal arranged for the transfer of the money. Peck did likewise.

G. Lee Greer

Chapter 7

As Peck pulled up to the entrance to what could only be described as a mansion in Georgetown, the home of the hostess, Mary Leigh Braxton, he was dreading the evening. This was the party of the year within the Beltway and people would kill for an invitation but the attendance was limited to 100 movers and shakers and their guests. That meant 201 people, counting the hostess and 202 was not admitted. If you were on the list for this party, you were perceived to be somebody very important to the goings on in Washington, D.C.

Peck liked the hostess but he had grown to dread most of the other company. At sixty two years of age, he had grown tired of this kind of life. The President was there, of course, as was the Vice-President, the congressional leadership, key cabinet members, a few foreign ambassadors, the military leadership, and lots of lobbyists. Any lobbyist not in attendance at this party was not considered to be seriously in the business.

The valet took Peck's car and he made his way inside, stopping to say hello and chat with those who greeted him. He made his way through the crowd and gave his drink order to one of the floating servers. He intended to make a reasonable and noticeable appearance and then get the hell out of there.

"Well, Peck, I see you decided to grace us with your presence and I will go ahead and admit it, I am glad you did," spoke Mary Leigh Braxton from behind Peck.

Peck turned and smiled at his hostess and said, "You are the only one who could get me out tonight and seeing you now, all decked out in your finest and you being the prettiest lady inside the beltway, tells me that I made a good decision. How are you, sweetheart?"

"I am fine, now that you are here. You do make a girl feel good about herself. I am going to have to move around a good bit tonight, but I want to spend some time with you, so don't try to sneak away without seeing me, Mary Leigh said as she kissed Peck on the cheek. With that, she fluttered away and Peck started moving through the crowd and caught the eye of the President, who motioned him over.

"Peck, even I, as President of the United States of America, cannot get Mary Leigh to kiss me on the cheek. How do you do that?" inquired the President.

"She is a good, long time friend, Mr. President, and was a good friend to my wife before we lost her. Mary Leigh is originally from my neck of the woods. We actually knew each other before she ended up here," offered Peck.

"I did not know that. She's one of a kind: a rich widow with more money than God, connected to everybody who is anybody in the beltway and without a doubt, the loveliest hostess in this town," said the President.

"She is more than that, Mr. President. She is a lovely person who, despite all the trappings, really cares about people," said Peck.

"I am sure she is, Peck. It's good to see you," the President said as he was being pressed for attention by others.

Peck wandered around and stopped among a group he heard discussing the recent demise of District Judge Josiah Hammond.

"It is frightening to consider that a federal judge could be killed because he is so controversial," spoke one of the group.

"Is there any evidence that he was killed because he was a federal judge? My understanding is that the authorities don't have a clue who killed him or why," interjected another. Have you heard anything, Peck?"

"No, only what I read in the papers but I understand that some people are trying to build the case that he was killed because of his far out opinions and based on his track record, I guess you could make a pretty good case. He certainly won't be missed from the bench. In my opinion, he was about as bad as they come and I hope that the people who recommend, appoint, and confirm his replacement will do so with the good of the country in mind and without political considerations. That is probably too much to ask for."

Peck made his way through the crowd and stopped among a small group, most of whom he knew and was greeted by all.

"Peck, Senator Folsom here has the opinion that the military is greatly over funded and needs to be checked," said one of the participants. "What do you say?"

"If anything, they are under funded but maybe, if we could eliminate some of these boondoggle projects that the military leadership does not want but which the members of Congress, in their infinite wisdom, insist on adding to the military appropriation in order to provide jobs and investment in their State and congressional districts, we might could get by with smaller increases," said Peck.

Senator Folsom reddened as he said, "The military budget could be cut twenty five percent today and we would not know the difference. We have too many weapon systems, too many ships and planes and too many people in uniform. They are out of control and too gung ho to jump into battle at the slightest provocation. They are not that important in the grand scheme of things."

Peck started to walk away, and he knew that he should, but he had to say something to this pompous, ill informed ass.

"One marine grunt, one dogface, one swabbie, or one airman, was yesterday, is today, and will be tomorrow more important to this great nation than every member who ever served in congress. They are the people who stand between us and evil. They are the guardians of liberty and democracy and afford the opportunity for people like you, Senator Folsom, to say such utterly ridiculous and irresponsible things. You should fall down on your knees every night and thank God that these people are willing to protect us, in spite of people like you," fired Peck.

"I strongly resent your tone and your words and I think that it would be in order for you to apologize to me and these other gentlemen," huffed Senator Folsom.

"You, Sir, are at a distinct disadvantage in this conversation" said Peck.

"And how is that?"

"Because you have obviously deluded yourself in to thinking that I give a good goddamn what you think," said Peck as he turned and walked away.

Peck wandered around trying to spot Mary Leigh to say his goodbye. He had to get out of that place. He finally spotted her and waited until she caught his eye and could gracefully get away and speak to him. As she approached him she noted his demeanor and knew that he was leaving.

"Okay, what has happened to make you want to leave me this early," inquired Mary Leigh.

"You read me pretty good and I sincerely apologize to you for asking to be excused but if I hang around here any longer I am going to smack somebody on the nose, embarrass you, and spoil your grand party," said Peck.

"Hell, Peck, if you will let me choose the nose I will give you a free swing and thank you for it. No apology is necessary and I just wish that I could leave with you. You are released from this asylum with the understanding and agreement that you will invite me down to your horse place, which you have promised to do more times than I care to remember," said Mary Leigh.

"That is a promise and I mean it. And now I will say goodnight, dear lady."

"Get out of here," said Mary Leigh as she bussed Peck on the cheek.

G. Lee Greer

As Peck drove away from the party he thought to himself how pleasant Mary Leigh was and he vowed to himself that he would invite her down to the horse place, as she called it, in the very near future.

Chapter 8

At his office, Peck removed his special phone from the locked drawer, entered his password, and keyed in speed dial one. The call was answered almost immediately with, "Yes."

"I think it's time to expand our list. I am thinking maybe seven candidates this time. Be thinking about a list of ten and I will get back to you later."

"Understood."

Peck keyed in the second party and said the same but added, "I think the three of us need to get together to sort all this out and I am thinking that your boat might be a good place to do it. What do you think?"

"Good idea. Why don't I see if I can set up a meeting? Are you pretty flexible for the next week or so?"

"Just let me know where and when and be prepared to discuss at least seven more candidates." Peck signed off.

The meeting was confirmed for two days later and they were gathered in the stateroom of a very sizeable yacht in the middle of Chesapeake Bay.

"Peck, I hear that you gave Senator Folsom a real dressing down the other night. I got a blow by blow account of the conversation and I only wish I had been standing next to you to see the expression on his face. That SOB had it coming. I just wish the people of his home State knew him for what he really is but they keep sending the bastard back here term after term after term. It is fortunate for the country that most people don't pay any attention to him when he takes off on the military," said one of the attendees.

"Well, it made me feel good if nobody else. I guess I have been looking for the opportunity to tell off that arrogant asshole."

"Why don't we each jot down the names of ten candidates and then we will compare lists and see if there is any unanimity among our choices. Can we agree to choose seven?" said Peck.

They each nodded and wrote down their choices and then turned them over to Peck, who read them, looking for matches.

"We have agreement on five; Senator Cabot Spenser, attorney Robert Simmons, Congressman Terrence Driscoll, the Reverend Lincoln Johnson, and a social activist, Ms. Gwen Wiley," said Peck.

"We have a two out of three agreement on two more. They are Ben Goldstone and Charles Dunning," said Peck.

"Tell me about those two," said the one who had not named them.

"Ben Goldstone advertises himself as a Hollywood producer but he is nothing more than a purveyor of filth. He is big in porn, including child porn, and he has a large production and distribution network here at home and internationally. He has been indicted a couple of times but he's wriggled out of both charges, claiming freedom of artistic expression and first amendment rights," said Peck.

"Charles Dunning is a Nazi, pure and simple. He is an ignorant buffoon but clever enough with words to attract others of similar ilk. He even has a web site on which he has posted the names, addresses, and telephone numbers of women who have visited doctors who are known to perform abortions. It is pretty well established that those web postings have resulted in the murder of two women, one of whom who was not even interested in an abortion but was merely seeing her doctor for routine pre-natal care," said the other who had listed Dunning.

"I will bow to the wisdom of you two. They sound like deserving candidates."

"Since we are now in agreement, I will get things rolling." said Peck.

Back in his office in the Reynolds Commerce building, Peck picked up the phone and buzzed Vincent on the intercom. "I need to see you for a moment as soon as you are free."

Vincent entered shortly afterward with, "What's up, Boss."

"Vincent, here are the names and particulars on seven people. I want you to relay this information to our friend and, needless to say, destroy the list when finished," said Peck.

"Wow! We are really notching it up, aren't we?"

"Yes, we are and they are all very deserving."

Vincent returned to his office, removed his secure phone from the locked drawer and, after keying in his password, keyed in the speed dial number of Jack O'Neal. There was an immediate tone that told Vincent that he could not talk now but would be available to receive his call in thirty minutes. He called again in thirty minutes and after the security sequence was satisfied he said, "I have the names and particulars on seven people on whom you are requested to act."

"Damn, you people are dead serious, aren't you? No pun intended. Let's have them."

Vincent gave him the information and O'Neal replied, "We are certainly going to earn our money on these."

"Thank you for your prompt attention. Good day."

O'Neal studied the list of targets, what he knew about them, if anything, and their location. He wanted to spread the work evenly but he had to make sure that everything fit as well as possible. After awhile he had decided to assign Spenser and Dunning to Pam Wallace, Driscoll to Don Casciolini, Simmons and Johnson to Joe Rollins, and Wiley and Goldstone to Angela Robechek. He would make the calls tomorrow.

Chapter 9

Angela Robechek studied the sketchy information given to her on the two assigned targets. She had heard or read about them but knew very little about their activities. She noted that Gwen Wiley was in San Francisco and Ben Goldstone was right there in Los Angeles. She decided to concentrate on Goldstone first. She had a home address and a business address, a small, independent studio in Hollywood. She headed for the studio address first just to do a drive by and get a feel for the neighborhood. She didn't like what she saw. The studio offered little opportunity. The only entrance was through a guarded gate and she felt sure that even if she was able to get onto the lot the three buildings would be secured with only known persons admitted. She next headed to the address of his home. It was in a posh, upscale community consisting of mini-estates of three to four acres. Goldstone's mansion, like just about all the others, was gated and she noted security cameras mounted in two places covering the entrance. She then noted that there were bare hills directly behind the property and what appeared to be bike trails. She gauged the distance to be about a thousand yards. She skirted around the neighborhood and found a dirt road that appeared to go up into the hills. She decided to return later with a bike to check it out.

Angela was an accomplished dirt biker and she loaded up her wheels on the trailer and returned to the area behind Goldstone's neighborhood and unloaded. There were a few other bikers around so she just cruised around, taking a few jumps and acting like she belonged. She came to a halt to ostensibly take a breather and removed a small pair of Zeiss binoculars to survey the area. She spotted Goldstone's house easily because she had noted a unique cupola mounted on the roof during her drive by. There was a large swimming pool and garden area out back and she gauged the distance to be about a thousand yards as she had estimated earlier. All she needed was to get him out by the pool. It was Friday and she planned to return on Saturday, and Sunday, if necessary, in the hope that he would show himself. A photograph had been couriered to her so she knew her target.

On Saturday she decided to wait until the end of the day with the hope that any other bikers would clear out and give her free and unobserved movement. For her weapon she chose a Remington model 700, bolt action, with a bull barrel, 7.62 caliber, a Carswell silencer, and a flash suppressor. In case the shot had to be made after dark, she also threw in an infrared pack. She hoped to get in a dusk shot which was the preferred time. She arrived about one hour before dusk and was relieved to see that there were no bikers left on the hill. A quick survey of the residence revealed a lot of activity by the pool. It looked like a party was in progress. She returned to her vehicle for the weapon and then settled on a spot for the shot where she would be unobserved from below. She had also taken the precaution of installing a high suppression muffler on the bike so that her departure would not be detected.

It was nearing dusk as she readied her weapon and she used the scope to work the crowd until she spotted her target. He was surrounded by topless bimbos and wore a black silk shirt opened down to the navel and was wearing enough gold chains to qualify him as a pimp. Tacky bastard, she thought. He moved out next to the pool, standing alone, apparently addressing his party guests and she raised her weapon and sighted in. The crosshairs came to rest between his eyes and she exhaled slowly, stopped mid way, and pulled the trigger. He was flung into the pool as the party guests screamed and began scrambling in all directions, ducking for what cover they could find. Angela quickly loaded her weapon into the carrier, made her way back to the bike, loaded onto the trailer, and was clear of the area within minutes. Later she would remove the tires from her bike, destroy them, and replace them with a different tread. The barrel from the rifle would be replaced and dropped into deep water.

The police arrived ten minutes later. They would get around to the hill sooner or later, but she had left them with little to work with. The morning newspaper gave the story front page, but there was not much to report beyond his death.

Angela packed a bag and stored her weapons in a hideaway panel of her Ford

Expedition and headed for San Francisco. She took her time, stretching the trip into nearly three days. After checking into a motel, she checked her city map to find the street where Ms. Wiley lived. She found it and decided that she would begin her surveillance tomorrow.

Ms. Gwen Wiley, the savior of the endangered and oppressed, lived very well. She had grown up a pampered child in a well to do family. Apparently the pampering continued on, even through the nine years it took her to get her degree at Berkley. She lived on a sizeable annuity established by her father and flitted around the country and the world in support of all the great causes. If she wasn't saving whales, she was decrying the evils of nuclear energy, the automobile, fossil fuels, the environment, global trade, global warming, and any other chic cause of the day. She didn't bother to tell her friends in the movement that when she was at home, she tooled around town in a vintage Jaguar X-12, the biggest gas guzzler ever to hit the road. She lived comfortably in an upper middle class neighborhood,

Angela found the house and rode the neighborhood to get her bearings. She didn't even know if Ms. Wiley was in town. She stopped at a pay phone and dialed her number. It was answered after the third ring.

"Hi. Is this Ms. Gwen Wiley?"

"Yes. Who is calling, please?"

"You don't know me. My name is Suzzane Marshall and your name was given to me by a friend in Amsterdam who suggested that you were someone I needed to meet," said Angela.

"Why would you need to meet me?" asked Ms. Wiley.

"I am trying to organize a rally and demonstration at the Redwood National Forest to try to stop the proposed cutting of timber in the park and it was suggested to me that you were, far and away, the expert in these matters. I would appreciate it if you would give me about one hour this evening, if possible. I can come to your home or meet you anywhere you like if you can give me the time. If this evening is not convenient, I will meet you at your convenience. I will be in town for at least three more days."

"I have just returned from a trip and had not planned to go out this evening. Why don't you come around to my home around eight o'clock? Do you know how to get here?"

"No. I am in the middle of downtown and would appreciate directions."

Directions were given and Angela signed off with, "Thank you so much for giving me the time. I will see you around eight."

Angela returned to her motel, ordered room service, and packed her bag. She planned to be on the road headed south by eight fifteen. After eating, she went out to the vehicle to choose her weapon. Since she planned for this job to be up close and personal, she chose a Browning 9mm with a silencer. She placed the weapon in a tote bag and waited for the appointed time.

She parked her vehicle a block away and walked to Ms. Wiley's residence. She rang the doorbell and shortly the door was opened by Ms. Wiley.

"Come in, Suzzane. I'm Gwen Wiley."

"It is an honor to meet you. I have heard so many good things about you."

Ms. Wiley led the way back to a sitting area and went behind a small bar. Angela took a seat in front of the bar with her tote bag in her lap.

"May I get you something to drink?"

"No. I really don't have the time."

"I have all evening to devote to you," said Ms. Wiley.

"No. You don't," said Angela as she pulled the Browning from her tote bag, reached across the bar and shot her gracious host between the eyes. After checking to make sure her victim was dead and retrieving the spent casing, she exited the home.

Angela looked at her watch as she entered her car and it was eight ten as she began her return trip south.

Two days later, Jack O'Neal arranged for the transfer of the money and so did Peck. Angela was talking with a real estate agent and looking at horses.

Chapter 10

Don Casciolini studied the brief file of Congressman Terrence Driscoll. He knew him and had even met him some years earlier. Driscoll was an extreme, left wing radical, and a closet homosexual, even though he had a wife. He had strong ties to the IRA and was constantly trying to justify their actions. As a matter of fact, he seemed to be the number one apologist for terrorists of every stripe. He never saw a government program he did not like and the bigger and more costly, the better.

Don noted in the newspaper that the Congressman was back in the district for a few days and had scheduled a rally/fundraiser for the coming weekend. Since it was open to the public and there would be a large crowd, Don decided to attend.

The rally was as advertised with plenty of food and drink. Driscoll worked the crowd and as Don noticed him working his way toward him, a plan of action sprang into mind.

"Hi. I'm Terrence Driscoll and I appreciate you coming out today," he said as he extended his hand.

Don grasped his hand into both of his and said, "Hello. I am Tony Furrillo and I am a long time fan of yours. It is an honor to meet you."

Still holding his hand Don looked directly into his eyes and continued, "I would love to have the opportunity to meet privately with you sometime and discuss with you how I might be of service."

Driscoll, withdrawing his hand studied Don for a moment and then said, "I think that maybe that would be beneficial to both of us but it is difficult for me to get free."

"I understand."

Driscoll started to walk away but he stopped and turned around and said, "Are you familiar with the stretch of beach just north of the point? Sometimes I like to go there alone late at night to gather my thoughts and I was thinking that maybe after today's full schedule I will need to relax a little tonight. Say ten o'clock."

"I look forward to it."

As Driscoll continued to work the crowd, Don made his way home to lay out his plan. He decide to use a Thompson Contender hand cannon, 50 caliber, with a 15 inch barrel, a two power scope with night vision, a flash suppressor, and a silencer. This would give him an effective range of fifty yards and allow him to maintain a distance in case there were others out on the beach.

He arrived at the beach thirty minutes early and parked about a half mile from the meeting point. He took off his shoes, left them in the car, and began strolling down the beach. His weapon was easily carried in a pack slung over his shoulder. He came to an outcropping of boulders down at the water line and at low tide he was able to get in among them completely out of view. He figured that he was about one hundred yards from where Driscoll would enter the beach. Around ten o'clock he noted car headlights approaching from up the road and it came to a stop, the lights were cut and he heard the car door slam. Driscoll was about seventy five yards away as he walked down to the water line of waves rushing in. Don already had him sighted in his night scope but he needed him closer to make it a sure, clean shot. Driscoll stopped, looked up and down the beach, and started walking the other way.

Don spoke as loudly as he could without yelling, "Congressman, is that you?"

Yes," he said and started walking in the direction of the voice.

Don kept him focused and as Driscoll was nearly forty yards away, he fired. Driscoll recoiled backward onto his back. Don focused in again to make sure that he was dead. He did not want to approach the area of the body. Seeing the entry wound between the eyes satisfied him that his quarry was dead. He put his weapon in the carryall and strolled back up the beach to his car.

The body was discovered the next morning by early morning beach strollers.

G. Lee Greer

Chapter 11

United States Attorney General Edmund Stevens had called the meeting in his office. Present with him were John Talbot, Director of the FBI and Deborah Craig, Assistant Attorney General for civil rights.

"Let me begin by saying that at this point in time nothing we say here today is to be discussed with anyone else for any reason and that includes your closest staff. We may or may not have anything to be concerned with, but it deserves a look, just in case," said the Attorney General.

Talbot and Craig had no idea what he was talking about but said nothing.

"What we have are four dead people, Judge Josiah Hammond of Buffalo, New York, Congressman Terrence Driscoll, of Boston, Mr. Ben Goldstone, Hollywood, and Ms. Gwen Wiley, of San Francisco, seemingly unrelated, but which have a couple of things in common. Number one: they were all murdered, execution style, and it would appear to be professional hits. Number two: They were all hard aport on the political spectrum. They were what could be described as radical left wingers. If they had gone any further left they would have fallen off the map," said the Attorney General.

"What prompted the Justice Department's interest in this?" asked FBI Director Talbot.

"It was brought to me by one of my staff attorneys who had been reviewing the file on Judge Hammond and who had heard of the others in the news. He made some discreet inquiries to some contacts in Boston, San Francisco, and Los Angeles on the particulars of the other three deaths and decided to bring it to me. I have decided that it deserves a preliminary look," answered Stevens.

"Has there been any complaint or suggestion from anyone outside of Justice?" asked Assistant Attorney General Craig."

"No and let's hope that it stays that way for awhile, at least until we can get some idea what we may or may not be dealing with. The media has not picked up on it yet but they will, sooner or later, and when they do every conspiracy nut in the country is going to come out of the woodwork and offer their expert opinions on every radio and TV talk show in the country. All the talking heads on television will start wringing their hands in anguish and all the politicians will get into the act and we will find ourselves covered up and won't be able to work on anything else until it dies down," said Stevens.

"John, we have the file on Judge Hammond since we have jurisdiction on that one and I want you to build a file on the other three as discreetly as possible. Deborah, you will review the files along with John because if this thing does develop into a conspiracy or even if someone is acting alone and these people were targeted for political reasons, your division would take the lead on any federal prosecution that might result," continued Stevens.

Stevens arose from his chair, signaling the end of the meeting, and said, "Remember mum's the word until we can get our arms around this thing and decide whether we have something here or not."

When John Talbot returned to his office he picked up the phone and called his lead agent in Boston and said, "Sid, I want you to very discreetly find out everything you can about the murder of Congressman Driscoll and I stress the word discreet. Use your contacts inside Boston police and build as complete a file as possible. This file is for my eyes only and you're not to discuss this matter with anyone. When you have it, courier it down to me marked for my eyes only."

Subsequent calls to San Francisco and Los Angeles followed.

G. Lee Greer

Chapter 12

Pam Wallace had been given the names of two targets and a brief file on each had been forwarded. Charles Dunning lived downstate Illinois in the small town of Pelham. Senator Cabot Spenser maintained a residence in Madison, Wisconsin when he wasn't in Washington. She knew that summer recess was coming up soon and he would be back in the State grabbing hands, patting backs, and laughing at inane remarks of his constituents, so she decided to concentrate on Charles Dunning first.

She drove downstate to Pelham, primarily a farming community of about twenty five hundred people, dotted with silos everywhere and a couple of small manufacturing concerns. The sign at the city limits said, "Welcome to Pelham, the friendliest little city in the USA." To Charles Dunning that applied if you were white, protestant, blonde headed, and hated abortionists. Pam angle parked a few doors down from the front of a building called the Pelham Café. She figured that this was a good place to start as the cafés all across America were notorious as havens of gossip.

Upon entering she noted that the place was almost empty and she took a seat at the counter and picked up a menu. She was greeted by the waitress who said, "Hello, stranger, I'm Sally, the best waitress in the Pelham Café. I am also the only waitress and also the owner of this little enterprise. Would you like to buy it?"

With a broad smile, Pam said, "No, I'm just passing through, taking the scenic route down to Nashville. I hate interstate highways."

"A girl after my own heart. What can I get you, honey?"

"How about a BLT and some sweet iced tea?"

"Coming up."

When Sally brought her order, Pam said, "So, Sally, what is Pelham's claim to fame, anything or anyone notable?"

"Oh yeah, we are full of it. We grow more corn per acre than anywhere else in the country, we've got the oldest continuously operated blacksmith shop in America and we've got a nut job named Charles Dunning, who lives a couple of miles out of town, and who is going to save the world. Other than that we are pretty normal."

"How is this Mr. Dunning planning on saving the world?"

"Oh, he's got it all figured out. If he can just rid the world of all non-white people, all the Jews, all the Roman Catholics, and all the doctors who perform abortions, we will all live in paradise; a real heaven on earth," answered Sally.

"You don't sound like you are a member of his fan club."

"You could say that. I threw him out of here one time and told him never to come back and if he did he wouldn't leave here walking."

"Does he have much of a following around here?"

"Some. I would say about twenty percent but most of them are classified as borderline morons."

"What does his family think about him?" asked Pam.

"He doesn't have much family left. He's a bachelor. His wife ran off and took the kids with her about five years ago and no one has heard from her since. He has a brother over in the next town but he doesn't have anything to do with him anymore. He lives out there near the old sawmill all by his lonesome and that suits the hell out of most of the people in this town. The less we see of him, the better."

"Well, Sally. I have enjoyed our little visit. You've got a nice little place here and the sandwich and tea were great but it is going to be dark soon and I would like to get a few more miles on down the road before I stop for the night. If I come back by the same route I will make a point to stop in and visit with you again."

"You take care, honey. If you are heading south to Nashville, just stay straight right on out of town. A couple of miles out of town you will pass the old sawmill and the Dunning place. If he's outside, toot the horn at the crazy sonofabitch. You come back now."

Pam returned to her car and sat there a few moments thinking. She decided that she would stop by to see Mr. Dunning and if anyone was around she would just ask directions and move on. At least it would give her the opportunity look at the lay of the land and plan her action. She drove on out of town for about a mile and then pulled over to the side of the road and stopped. She released the trunk latch and got out of the car and after moving a few things around she retrieved her pistol, a 38 special, attached the silencer and got back in the car. Her oversized handbag was large enough to hide the suppressed weapon. As she slowly rode on down the road, she caught sight of what had to be the old sawmill and there was a house sitting behind it about fifty yards. That had to be the Dunning place. As she pulled off the road at the sawmill road she noted that there was one vehicle, a pickup truck, parked in front of the house. She pulled in behind it, exited the car and as she was climbing the stairs to the porch, the screen door opened and a large man, unshaven and generally unkempt, said, "What can I do for you?"

Pam acted startled and said, "Sorry for coming up unannounced. I was looking for Mr. Charles Dunning."

"I'm Charles Dunning but if you're selling, I ain't buying."

"Well, then I've stopped for nothing. I was hoping to talk with you about your web site. I have a small company that deals in web site development and maintenance and I know that you contract out your site work. I have visited your web site and it is pretty good but I have some ideas that I think would make it a lot more appealing and serviceable and can probably provide you with a better service, including quicker updates, and at a very competitive price."

"What's your name?"

"I'm Sarah Windham."

Dunning looked her over closely from head to toe, obviously admiring the attractive woman in front of him and Pam was sure that he was not thinking about websites. Let the ugly sonofabitch gawk all he wants if it will just get me inside with him, she thought.

"Would you like to come in, Miss Windham?"

"Thank you, but if it is not convenient, if you're expecting anyone, I can come back tomorrow."

"No, I'm not expecting anyone. You just come on in and we will talk about your services."

Dunning opened the screen door and allowed her to enter first. What a dump, she thought. It sure fits him.

"Can I get you anything to drink, Sarah? I was just getting ready to have myself a drink and I can fix two if you like."

"A soda would be nice if it is not too much trouble."

"I'll be right back."

When he went into the kitchen Pam removed the weapon from her handbag and held it behind her back. As Dunning returned she pulled the weapon out and up and shot him between the eyes. He crumpled to the floor and Pam knew he was dead but she put another round into his temple and with that there wasn't much of his head left.

Pam then stood there motionless for what seemed like a long time, dazed from the realization of what she had done and how easy it had been. She had never killed anyone before except in the line of duty and she felt her stomach growing queasy and she rushed from the house. She took a number of deep breaths to calm herself and then her mind took over with her plan for exiting the scene. She didn't want to risk going back through town and she decided to continue on south for about a hundred miles, then catch route 64 west towards St. Louis and then turn back north on route 55 to Chicago.

    She pulled out on to the highway, heading south unobserved. It would be nearly a week before the body was found. Charles Dunning had no friends who cared to check up on him and if the newspapers hadn't started piling up on the porch he could have gone for months without being found.

Chapter 13

Joe Rollins decided to take on the assignment of the Reverend Lincoln "The Mouth" Johnson first, figuring it to be a harder job than the other target. Studying the file, he learned that Johnson spent most of his time in New York but that he also maintained an apartment in Washington. He would have no problem recognizing his target since "The Mouth" was constantly all over the TV complaining about one thing or another trying to stir people up so that they would drop some coin in his coffers to enable him to continue his noble struggle on behalf of the people. It was a standing joke among some in the black community that if you saw "The Mouth" on TV you knew that his bank account was getting low in funds and that without a cause to part some innocent souls from their money he would have to get a real job or panhandle. He wasn't as sophisticated as another high profile, so called civil rights leader who maintained a steady program of legalized extortion to keep the funds rolling in on a regular basis.

Joe headed north on I-85 planning, to spend a few days nosing around Harlem to pick up what he could on Johnson's movements. After traveling most of the day, he decided to overnight in D.C. and check out the neighborhood of Johnson's apartment. He checked into a motel, showered, changed clothes and returned to his car to survey the area. He quickly located the address given him and took mental notes of ingress and egress avenues. After satisfying himself that he had done all he could at that time he stopped at a local bar about a block away from the apartment.

He entered the dimly lit establishment with a long bar extending the entire length of the right side of the room, with booths lining the left side. There was a small dance area down at the end of the room with a jukebox nearby. There was also a small bandstand close by so apparently they enjoyed live entertainment occasionally. He took a seat at the bar, which was empty except for him, the bartender and a couple sitting snugly in one of the booths. The guy was using his best routine trying to work up a little action with the lady and it was obvious she wasn't buying but she let him buy her as many drinks as he wanted to.

"What can I get you, friend?" said the bartender.

"A cold draft, please."

"I'm Freddie, said the bartender as he drew the draft. I don't believe I've seen you around before."

"Haven't been around in a long time. I'm Joe Simms from Baltimore," Joe said as he extended his hand across the bar.

"Do you serve food here?" Joe continued.

"I can serve up almost anything you want as long as it's a cheeseburger, but I'll guarantee you that it will be the best damn cheeseburger you ever had, with homemade french fries too. None of that frozen crap. You know, most of the kids today will go through their whole life and never know what a real french fry tastes like, and that's a shame. If you don't agree with me about it being the best, you don't pay me. Now you can't beat a deal like that."

"You're right. I'll have the cheeseburger and another draft."

Freddie called to the back saying, "Give me one of your best, Bessie."

Freddie read the newspaper while he was waiting on the cheeseburger order and Joe sat in silence, sipping his draft beer.

"Oh, shit. I see that "The Mouth" is in town. I wonder what that con artist is hustling up today," noted Freddie.

"The Mouth?"

"Yeah. You don't know "The Mouth," the Right Reverend Lincoln Johnson, man of the people and the biggest con artist since P.T. Barnum?"

"I've never had the pleasure but I've heard of him. Do you know him?" asked Joe.

"I know the bastard real well. He's been in here a few times, sporting a honey on each arm and running his fat mouth when he's not filling it with booze. What burns me is that he will leave here, go around the corner to the local congregation and lay some shit on them about his latest struggle for the people and those little mothers and grandmothers will throw their dollars at him and then he'll walk back here with his pockets stuffed with cash, buy a round for the house before leaving with his women. He loves his women. They say he don't go nowhere without a piece of ass within grabbing distance. Everybody with an ounce of brains knows what a phony he is but we all let him get by with it because he's always being criticized by white folk and we don't want them to know that we think they're right about anything."

"What does the paper say his reason is for being in town?"

"Something about him demonstrating on the Capitol steps until Congress agrees to appropriate more money for poor people. What a shithead. He'll be around long enough to fill his pockets with cash and then he'll be on his way," said Freddie.

"Here's your cheeseburger."

"Thanks."

Joe ate his cheeseburger in silence and decided to go on up to Harlem tomorrow and nose around for a couple of days. Maybe he would meet up with "The Mouth" up there.

After finishing the cheeseburger, Joe said, "You were right, Freddie. That is the best cheeseburger I've ever had. I'm glad I stopped in and I enjoyed meeting you. It's nice to meet a man who tells it straight. I'll stop in again if I'm in the neighborhood."

After a good nights rest, Joe continued his trip up to New York and drove down to the Port Authority building, parked his car in a rental garage and walked two blocks to a car rental agency. He rented a car, using his Connecticut identity and drove down to Harlem. After finding a place to stay, he started making the rounds, chatting up the locals and trying to work "The Mouth" into the conversation without seeming interested. It seemed that everyone had a story and an opinion about Johnson. There was no middle ground. They either liked him or detested him. He also visited with a real estate agency and made inquiry about rentals and possible apartments or condominiums for sale. He told the agent that he was considering moving to New York. He needed a reason for being there in case his presence was noted later on.

He went by Johnson's condominium building, a nice six story structure which sort of stood out in the neighborhood. He noted that the entrance was manned by what had to be a rent-a-cop and no one was getting in except those who belonged or had other business there. He went around the corner to find the parking garage entrance and noticed that it was unmanned but controlled by an overhead steel door with an electronic card entry. He was sure that the card would also control an elevator inside the garage. He needed to pay Mel a visit.

Mel, also known as "the technician," was a free lance electronics wizard who operated out of his second story walkup apartment in Manhattan, just off 42nd street. He had a large clientele, including government agencies, private detectives, almost anyone who could pay the price for his expertise. Joe had used him before and he was confident that Mel could solve his problem.

Joe rang the bell at Mel's place and as he stood there he was being screened by Mel's video camera which was linked to his computer seeking a digital match of his image with the files. The computer signaled a match and Mel opened the door.

"Come in. It has been awhile since you have paid me a visit. What can I do for you?" said Mel.

"Hello, Mel. It is good to see you. I need to gain entry to a location that uses an electronic card reader," replied Joe.

"Describe it to me."

"It is a post mounted panel, about a foot square with what appears to be three light signals. The user holds the card in front of the panel and the reader accepts or rejects."

"That device uses a low level radio signal. The first light denotes the presence of the card, the second light denotes the reading of the card and the third light signals okay or reject and activates the control," said Mel as he moved across the room and retrieved a small device from the shelf and returned to Joe.

"Take this with you and get within fifty yards of the reader. Here is the on switch. When a user approaches, turn it on and point the front in the general direction of the panel. It will read the user's card when they use it. Bring it back to me and I will burn you a card just like the card used."

"Thanks, Mel. How late will you be up tonight?"

"Anytime up to midnight."

"I'll probably see you tonight."

Joe returned to the parking garage and parked as near the entrance as possible. In a short time a lady drove up to the entrance and lowered her window in front of the panel. Joe had switched the reader unit on and was pointing the unit as the lady held her card in front of the panel. Joe's reader lit up and the garage door slowly opened. Joe had his read. He would return later with his card and test it out.

Joe spent the next day around the neighborhood and found out that "The Mouth"

JUSTICE REGAINED

had a favorite place to hang with the sisters and brother called the Gentlemen's Club. He would visit there tonight.

Joe entered the Gentlemen's Club about nine o'clock that evening. The place was about half full with a trio playing modern jazz. Joe didn't care much for modern jazz: it didn't seem to have a melody and you could play any notes you wanted and no one would know the difference. Joe was a jazz purist. He ordered a draft and chatted with the bartender briefly about nothing in particular.

"Kinda slow tonight, isn't it?" Joe said.

"Yeah. It'll pick up some later on when the after dinner crowd starts wandering in. By midnight you won't be able to stir them with a stick and if "The Mouth" comes in with his entourage it'll really start hopping. Don't think he will be in tonight though. I heard he was down in D.C. stirring things up," said the bartender.

Joe had one more draft and decided to leave and go by the parking garage and check out his new card. He drove up to the garage door and held his newly minted card in front of the panel. The door slowly opened and he drove on in and found an unmarked parking space. He needed to check the card for the elevator entry. Exiting his car and walking to the elevator he noted a parking space designated Rev. Lincoln Johnson and that the space was empty. Apparently "The Mouth" had not returned from D.C.

Joe held his card in front of the panel mounted next to the elevator and was pleased when the door opened. He decided to take a chance and gain entry to Johnson's apartment hoping that he was right about him being out of town. He knew from the file that Johnson lived alone, having been divorced some years earlier. He pushed the button for the fifth floor and upon exiting the elevator began looking for his target's condo. The rooms were not numbered but the doors were labeled with a brass plate etching of the name of the occupant. Upon finding Johnson's condo he took out his picks to defeat the lock and in a matter of seconds he heard the click and turned the knob. Upon entering the dark room he took out his penlight, turned it on and began a survey of the area. There was a large living room, a kitchen/dining area and two bedrooms. He determined which of the bedrooms was the master suite, and figuring that he had the layout solidly set in his mind, he exited the condo and made his way back to the elevator and down to the garage. He exited the garage by pushing the release button at the garage door exit.

The next night Joe was back at the Gentlemen's Club, arriving about ten o'clock. The place was in full swing and from the noise and laughter he quickly spotted "The Mouth" and his party. He ordered a draft and observed Johnson's party having a grand time. All of a sudden Joe heard glass breaking, chairs sliding and he saw two women crawling around on the floor, pulling each others hair and scratching. It was a real cat fight and Johnson just stood there glaring at them. The combatants were soon pulled apart, still screaming threats and obscenities at each other,

"Both of you whores get out of my sight," screamed Johnson.

"But I want to be with you tonight," sobbed one of the women.

"Get them out of my sight," Johnson ordered one of his assistants who quickly hustled the women from the room, still kicking and screaming.

For the rest of the evening "The Mouth" just sat there sullenly, drinking his booze, seemingly oblivious to the frivolity around him and shortly after midnight he left the club alone. Joe waited for about a half hour and then exited. He planned to strike tonight but he wanted to give his target plenty of time to settle in and into a sound sleep.

At about three o'clock in the morning Joe drove up to the garage door of Johnson's building, held his card up to the panel and when the door slowly opened he entered the garage, parked his car and took the elevator up to his target's condo. He quickly gained entry to the condo with his picks and after closing the door behind him, stood silently listening for any sounds of life. He could hear the loud snoring coming from the master bedroom as he crept into the room. There was enough light streaming in from the street for Joe to see that Johnson was sprawled on top of the bed, without any cover and completely naked. Joe slid the knife, a Japanese made Kuban knife, with a seven inch blade, paper thin and sharp as a scalpel, from the sheath and made his way to the side of the bed. Johnson was lying on his stomach and with a quick motion Joe grabbed his hair, lifting his head upward and slit his throat from ear to ear. There was no sound except the gurgling noise of the victim gasping for air which would not come. Joe waited for a couple of minutes to assure himself that his target was dead, then wiped his blade on the bed covers and stole from the room and the condo. He returned to the garage, left as he had come and returned to his motel.

The next morning Joe Rollins slept late, had a leisurely breakfast, checked out of the motel, retrieved his car, and hit I-95 heading south to Atlanta.

The body was discovered in the afternoon and when it hit the news, Jack O'Neal made arrangement for the transfer of the money.

Chapter 14

Attorney General Edmund Stevens had called another meeting with FBI Director John Talbot and Assistant Attorney General Deborah Craig.

"People, we have one, possibly two more to add to our list. Lincoln Johnson, for sure and maybe Charles Dunning, although he doesn't fit the complete profile. He's as far right wing as the other five are left wing but I don't want to rule him out. Maybe our killer or killers are equal opportunity assassins. The talk is starting and I am going to brief the President today on what we have, which is nothing more than a suspicion. John, I need for you to start files on these latest two victims and have your people find out everything that the local jurisdictions have come up with," said Stevens.

When the meeting broke up, the Attorney General made his way over to the White House for his meeting with the President. He was ushered right in and he got right to the point.

"Mr. President, what I am going to tell you may or may not have any basis but, in my opinion, it has progressed far enough to warrant telling you what I think so that you don't get caught off guard," said Stevens.

"Let's hear it, Edmund."

"Mr. President, there is a possibility that we have an individual or a group who are out knocking off people for other than personal reasons. It could be political."

"What on earth are you talking about, Edmund?"

The Attorney General recounted all of the information that he had to date and posed the theory that these could be political assassinations and not just random coincidence.

"That is incredible, Edmund. Do you really think that there is a conspiracy afoot to kill off all the extremists in this country? If so, they have a long way to go and a lot of bodies to pile up," said the President.

"I must stress, Mr. President, that it is only a possibility but I felt I needed to brief you in case someone else comes up with the same theory and starts talking about it," said Stevens.

"Of course, Edmund, and I appreciate it. You keep me updated, if necessary."

Chapter 15

Pam Wallace was studying the file on Senator Cabot Spenser. He was the senior senator from the State of Wisconsin, chairman of the judiciary committee and a member of the senate finance committee. He was a silver spooned millionaire with old family money and had held one political office after another since he was twenty four years of age. He had never held a real job in his life but he was the self appointed champion of the working man and woman although he had no clue what these people dealt with on a daily basis. He was the far left's darling and had presidential ambitions, but he was too far left even for most of the members of his own party. He was an admitted obstructionist as chairman of the judiciary committee and used every tactic available to keep conservative or moderate judges off the bench. His own committee had overridden his objections on a few occasions, when his tactics were so demonstrably obstructionist and the nominee was popularly supported in the senate. The latest nominee's name, to which Spenser had objected, had been forwarded to the full senate and had been approved by a vote of 97 to 3. That is how out of touch he was but he had a loyal core following in his home state and had been elected and reelected four times.

Pam noted that he would be returning to the State in a few days for the summer recess and would be there for almost three weeks. He had scheduled a number of public appearances at events of his liking. She decided to visit a couple of the sites where he was scheduled to appear and see what the possibilities were.

The first was in Racine where he was to mix and mingle with the people during a local company's family picnic. It was to be held at a large city park and the crowd was expected to number around five thousand. She found the park and drove around the perimeter looking for potential cover. She determined that the park was so thick in trees that it would be difficult to find a spot with enough open area to give her a long range shot, and she didn't cater to the idea of up close work with so many people around. She discounted Racine and went on to Madison to check out a convention hall where one of the appearances was scheduled and his home. She quickly ruled out the convention hall because of limited ingress and egress and took a look at his home in an upscale neighborhood just outside the city. The home was completely surrounded by a ten foot stone wall and gated, with security hut discreetly built nearby. She was sure that there would be dogs roaming the grounds too and she didn't like the feel of the surroundings.

She found a motel, checked in, and bought the local newspaper. Over her room service dinner, she scanned the local paper and found a reference she thought might give her the opportunity she needed to get the job done. In a column of local interest she noted that, according to the writer, Senator Spenser, after a number of whirlwind public appearances, planned to retreat to his family vacation home on Lake Geneva for about ten days of much needed rest. The public was encouraged to respect the Senator's privacy and allow him to relax.

The next morning she was on her way to Lake Geneva, about a two mile drive from Madison. Upon arriving at the lake she stopped at a local store which sold everything from groceries to boat oars to fish bait. She browsed around until the other two patrons had departed and then engaged the clerk or owner in conversation.

"I am looking for some information about house rentals and wondered if you could steer me in the right direction," Pam said.

"Sure can. My daughter runs a rental and sales agency right down the road about a mile. If there is anything available, she will know about it. Look for it on the right. It's called the Lakeshore Agency. My daughter's name is Merle," offered the clerk.

"Thanks. You have been a big help."

Pam continued on down the road to the Lakeshore Agency and when she entered she was greeted with, "Hello. I'm Merle. May I help you?"

"Hi. I am Pat Vaughn. I am looking to rent a house on the lake for a month. I drove up here to look around. I used to visit up here when I was a child and remembered how quiet and serene the place was. Do you know of any property that might be available?"

"Sure do. Things have been slow this summer and I have a number of properties I can show you if you have the time."

"I have plenty of time. How about right now?"

"Sure thing. Let me ring up dad and tell him I'm going to roll over my phone line to him until I get back. The only help I have is out sick so I will have to lock up the place."

"Take your time."

Pam waited while Merle called her dad, wrote out a "be back" sign, and taped it to the door. As they got into Merle's vehicle Merle asked, "How big a place do you need?"

"Oh, not very big. It's going to mostly be just me with maybe a visit from my brother and his family for a few days. To tell you the truth, it will suit me just fine if they can't make it. I am looking to completely relax for a whole month, something I haven't done in years," said Pam.

"Since you don't need too large a place I won't waste our time looking at the larger places but that still leaves us with three or four possibilities. The smallest is going to be two bedrooms. We're going to be coming up on the first one right up here," said Merle as she drove on up about a hundred yards and turned on to a narrow drive.

Merle unlocked the back door and they entered. "This one is three bedrooms, a large great room with a nice fireplace, a screened in front porch with rockers and a boat dock. It rents for $2500.00 a month with a $500.00 security deposit, refundable when you leave."

"This is great and we may come back to it but I want to look at some others. I am sure they're all nice."

"They are and I would not want you to make up your mind until you have seen the other properties. It would not be fair to the owners and I would not be earning my money if I did not show them. Let's get on to the next one."

The next property was pretty much the same and they went on to the next one. "This one is my favorite. I've tried to buy it for myself but the owner won't consider selling. It's on a little cove and you don't get a lot of boat traffic down here. Waterskiing is prohibited on this part of the lake and you only get some small boat traffic of recreational fishers. Your nearest neighbor is across the cove there. That's Senator Spenser's place although he's hardly ever here. He is going to be here for a week or ten days this month but you would pretty much have the cove to yourself for most of the month," advised Merle.

"It is beautiful but I am not sure I want to get caught up in all the hubbub that these politicians seem to generate wherever they go. Let's go look at one more and then I will try to decide," said Pam.

The next property was further down the lake about a mile and it too was fairly secluded. It was much like the others but Pam thought for her purposes this might be the better choice. The previous house across the cove was certainly convenient but it was also very obvious that it would get a lot of attention when the Senator was killed.

"How much is this one?" asked Pam.

"Two thousand a month and a five hundred dollar security deposit," said Merle.

"Let's go back to your office and do the paperwork.

I am going to take this one."

After returning and reopening the office Merle started filling out the standard rental agreement when Pam said,

"You don't mind cash, do you?"

"I love cash and so does the owner. If you don't mind I can give you a ten percent discount if we keep it off the books but if you need the paperwork we will have to run it through the mill.

"Off the books is fine with me and I love to save money. Let's see, with the ten percent discount that comes to $2,250.00 including the deposit," said Pam as she counted out the money for Merle.

"When do you want to start your rental? I can give you up to five days."

"I will be back in two days and will drop by to pick up the key," said Pam as she shook Merle's hand.

"It's a pleasure doing business with you, Pat, and I look forward to your return," said Merle as they walked to the door.

As Pam drove back home to Chicago she began to devise her plan. She had not rented the house across the cove from the Senator's place but she intended to use the place for her shot. She had noticed that trees, with low lying limbs extended out over the water, lined the shore in front of the house. A small boat could be easily maneuvered back into the limbs affording complete cover. She hoped that the house did not get rented in the next couple of weeks but even if it did the spot could be used at night without the occupant ever knowing it. All she needed now was to choose her weapon.

Chapter 16

Pam was back at the lake two days later and she stopped by to see Merle and pick up the key to the rental house. She then made arrangements to rent a small fishing boat and have it ferried over to her rental house. After buying some groceries to stock the kitchen she made her way to the rental house and settled in. She spent the rest of the day lying out on the dock reading and observing the activity on the lake. That night she stayed on the dock until after midnight to try to determine if she would encounter any night fishers and where they would likely be, if there at all. A few small boats came by but they were all gone by one o'clock.

The next morning, after her breakfast of cereal and a banana, she donned her fisherman's outfit, including a wide brimmed floppy hat, and loaded her bait and tackle into the boat. The boat had a small 35hp Johnson outboard motor with an electric trolling motor, as she had requested. She started up the outboard and went out on to the lake. She intended to do a lot of fishing in the cove where the Senator's house was located and she needed to survey the shoreline. After about a half mile down towards the cove, she cut the outboard and engaged the electric motor. She slowly made her way down the cove on the opposite bank from the Senator's house, casting her line toward the bank and slowly reeling it in. When she neared the cottage across the cove from the Senator, she deliberately cast her line a little long, snagging it in the low lying tree limbs. She slowly worked her way toward the snag, pulling her boat into the limbs to retrieve her hooked line. She found that with just a little effort she could move her boat completely behind the cover of the limbs. She also noted a large tree stump at the water line which she could easily use as a stable shooting platform. It would be a simple matter to step from the boat onto the stump. After releasing her hooked line she moved out from the bank, raised her electric motor, and started the outboard. She rode back up the cove at a slow speed, trying to etch in her mind everything she could. She intended to make a night run that night, because if the conditions were favorable, she intended to make a night shot.

Around ten o'clock that night, Pam got in the boat, started the outboard, and began the short mile run down to the cove. She used a small running light in case there were other boats in the area. About halfway down she cut the outboard and turned on the electric trolling motor and drifted down the cove. She noted a couple of houses with lights on but the Senator's house was still dark. She maneuvered her boat in and around the area in front of the house where she intended to make her shot. Although it was a moonlit night she pulled out her night vision goggles to survey the shoreline and the Senator's house. There were numerous trees in the yard between the bank and the house, but it was a fairly open area. She intended to wait for the Senator to come outside before she struck. Pam heard muttered voices nearby and saw a small two man boat making its way by about fifty yards away and quickly put down her glasses, picked up her rig and cast out of the boat toward the shore line. She knew that they would have seen her running light but that they would assume she was just another fisherman like themselves. When the other boat cleared the area she resumed her surveillance of the area until she was satisfied that she had a clear picture in her mind of the plan and the potential problems that might develop.

    The next morning Pam rode over in the boat to a local eatery where she had rented the boat and had breakfast. She bought a local paper and scanned it for weather and moon cycle information. She was looking for the moonless period and noted that it came during the middle of next week. When she returned to her house she called her brother and after explaining that she had felt the need to get away and relax and had rented the house on the lake, invited him and his family to come up for a week in about ten days. She also suggested that he call their dad and try to get him to come along. She would call him also and maybe between the two of them they could budge him from the house from which he rarely strayed since their mom had passed away. Her brother seemed to be excited about the idea and promised to get back to her. She gave him her cell number.

    Pam spent the next few days doing some serious fishing. She was good at it and each day she would take her catch back to the marina and either give the fish away or have some cleaned for her to cook up. She received a call from her brother telling her that they were coming but it would be two weeks before they could get away. Dad was coming too. Pam hoped that her job would be completed before they arrived. Their presence could put a real kink in her plans.

Each night Pam would take the boat out and ride down to the cove. This night she noted lights on at the Senator's house but she didn't know if he had arrived or someone was just readying the place. The next day she rode over to the marina and the café to listen for any word of the Senator's arrival but there was no mention of him. Her two night moonless period was coming up in three days and she hoped that he would arrive soon.

On Saturday, while Pam was at the marina, the Senator arrived and immediately began holding court for his subjects by regaling them with all the grand things he was doing for them and the country. Pam stood and listened along with the others for as long as she could take it and then quietly slipped away along with two or three of the locals. As they exited the establishment one of the locals said, "Now I remember why we keep sending that asshole back to Washington every time: so that he can't stand around here and spout that horseshit he feeds us. Pompous bastard!"

Pam had chosen a M1A (14) sniper rifle as her weapon, equipped with a night scope, noise suppressor, flash suppressor, and an infrared pack. It was sighted in and good for up to a thousand yards. She estimated that her shot would be no more than one hundred fifty yards.

She had decided to wait until Wednesday night for her first try; the first moonless night. With no lights behind to highlight her, she should be invisible on the lake.

On Wednesday night Pam started up the electric motor around 10:00 PM. She would be running without lights and it would be slow going but the battery was fully charged and she only had about two miles total round trip plus idling time. It didn't take her long to reach her destination and when she arrived she maneuvered her boat back among the overhanging tree limbs and noted that all the lights at the Senator's house, inside and out, There was obviously a party going on, judging from the number of people and the noise they generated. She left her weapon lying in the bottom of the boat and used her night vision binoculars to view the scene. Most of the people were out on the front porch and a few out in the yard. There was a bar setup on the porch and the booze was flowing freely. She spotted the Senator fondling some sweet young thing's ass and laughing uproariously. She had no interest in taking a shot in these surroundings so she settled down in the boat to wait it out. At one o'clock in the morning the party was still going strong and the Senator had disappeared inside. Pam decided to pack it in for the night and hope for the better tomorrow night. She turned her electric motor on and slowly made her way back to her place.

The next morning Pam put her battery for the electric motor on a slow charge and sat on the pier most of the day, occasionally waving to a passing motorist. Merle came by for a short visit and invited her to dinner, which she accepted, and in the afternoon she took a nap. She was at Merle's home by seven and enjoyed a pleasant dinner and conversation with her.

"You know, Merle, I just might be interested in buying up here. I have fallen in love with the place. Do you think that the owner of the house I am staying in might be interested in selling?" said Pam.

"There is nothing to lose in asking. I will get in touch with him and see if he is interested."

"Let me know what he says and now I need to get going. Thanks for the dinner and company," said Pam as she rose to leave.

"I enjoyed having you over and it would please me if you did buy a place up here. You fit in real well and you are well liked by the local folk," said Merle as she walked Pam to the door.

"Thanks again, Merle."

By ten o'clock Pam was sitting in the boat across from the Senator's house with the boat tied to a tree limb. There were lights on inside and out but no other signs of activity. Pam was viewing the scene with her night vision glasses. Later she heard voices, the noise easily carrying across the water and she noted that the Senator, another man, and sweet young thing were walking out into the yard. They walked down to the waters edge and in a few minutes, the other man, obviously an aide, discreetly made his way back inside. Pam had stepped out of the boat and was now sitting on the tree stump and was viewing the scene with her rifle scope as the Senator was holding a drink in one hand and alternating between fondling the breasts and squeezing the ass of sweet young thing with the other. Pam saw sweet young thing recoil from the Senator and rush back into the house. The Senator threw his drink glass at her as she fled. Pam wondered what he could have possibly have said to offend her.

Senator Cabot Spenser stood there, obviously disgruntled, and gazed out over the water. Pam had him sighted between the eyes and she took a deep breath, let it out halfway, and pulled the trigger. The Senator was flung backward, his head a scrambled mass of mush.

Pam stepped back into the boat, laid down her rifle, and threw the switch on the electric motor. Nothing happened. She had no power. She did not want to use the outboard motor with it's noise calling attention to her location and she didn't dare use her flashlight, fearful that someone would come outside and find the senator's body and any flash of light would pinpoint her location. She took up an oar and began making her way out into the cove and up the one mile to her place. The going was slow and she kept looking back to make sure that there was no activity underway at the senator's place. Her arms were tiring and as she got within about one hundred yards of her place she saw a running light on a boat sitting about twenty five yards off of her dock. She could not risk being seen docking at this time of the night so she rowed over near the bank and waited for the boat to be on its way. After a short while, she heard the outboard crank up and the boat sped on its way up the lake. Pam continued the last few yards to her dock, tied up the boat, and unloaded her weapon. Before entering the house, she stored her weapon in the hidden compartment of her vehicle. She would check out the electric motor in the morning.

The next morning, after a quick cup of coffee, Pam went out to the dock and the boat to check out the electric motor. She found one of the leads from the motor pulled loose from the battery post. She surmised that she had stepped on the lead while stepping on to the stump or when stepping back into the boat and pulled it loose. She reconnected the lead, started up the outboard and made her way over to the marina to have breakfast. As she was eating someone came in and told the crowd of the Senator's demise. His body had not been found until the next morning when the aide went looking for him. When he found the body he told sweet young thing what he had found and suggested to her that it would probably be the better part of discretion if she were not there when the police arrived. He would clear it with the police and she would need to be available later for a statement but he didn't want to face the wrath of Mrs. Spenser explaining her presence. He gave her enough time to throw her things together and leave, then he called the police.

Pam finished her breakfast and decided that she would fish off the pier today. The police called on everyone on the lake to see if anyone had seen or heard anything and Merle vouched for Pam and that was good enough for the local constabulary. Pam was looking forward to her brother and his family and dad's visit. She had less than three weeks left to enjoy the lake.

Chapter 17

Attorney General Edmund Stevens had just arrived at his desk when the phone rang.

"Sir, John Talbot is on line one. He says it's urgent," said the secretary.

"Good morning, John," Stevens said as he answered the phone.

"I'm afraid you're not going to think so when I give you the news. Senator Cabot Spenser was shot and killed last night."

"My office in one hour, John. I'll bring Deborah in also."

In one hour FBI Director John Talbot and Assistant Attorney General Deborah Craig entered the Attorney General's office and he opened the conversation with, "John, tell me what you know at this point."

"Senator Cabot was shot with what appears to be a high powered rifle in the front yard of his home on Lake Geneva. He was apparently killed sometime around midnight but wasn't discovered until this morning. I've got agents on the way up from Chicago and down from Milwaukee to lend any assistance we can to the local and state police. Even though he was a United States Senator we don't have jurisdiction. It is a local crime but I am sure that we can add Cabot to our list with the others, and, in my opinion, we need to begin assembling a task force and assume that there is a conspiracy to kill certain people for political reasons.

"I agree," chimed in Craig.

"I agree, too, but the task force will be assembled quietly and they will work in extreme secrecy at this point. Until we find something to tie this thing together we can't go public with a theory for which we have no substantiation or a hint of evidence. Give me the names of the people that you want on the task force and keep it as small as you can but cover all the bases. I want your recommendations by the end of the day. We will reconvene here at five o'clock. In the meantime I need to advise the President. See you at five."

"Mr. President, the Attorney General is on the line."

"Good morning, Edmund. I think I know what you are calling about. Senator Spenser, right?"

"Yes, Mr. President. I believe he fits the package and I wanted to advise you that I am quietly assembling a special task force to look into the conspiracy theory and see if we can get a handle on this thing."

"By all means, Edmund, and you keep me posted."

"Yes, Mr. President."

At five o'clock John Talbot and Deborah Craig were back at the Attorney General's office.

"All right, let's hear your recommendations," said Stevens.

"I would like to personally head up the special task force and, of course, there would be Deborah. I would also like to bring in Tom Garrison from our field office in Dallas. He is the best investigator in the Bureau. I would also like to recommend Bill Sisson, our number one forensics man, Jane Henson, who heads up our psychological department, and finally Ed Gorman, a former congressman, currently a lobbyist, and the most politically astute man I know," said Director Talbot.

"Isn't it a little risky to bring in an outsider at this point? I want this thing held close to the vest as long as we can. Can we rely on him to keep his mouth shut?" inquired Stevens.

"I know Gorman also and I believe that he is reliable and trustworthy," added Deborah Craig.

"We're talking about a former congressman, right? Stevens said with a grin and then added, I know Gorman, and I think he would be a good addition."

"All right. Get the team assembled and set up a meeting. Keep me advised of your activities. I will sit in on as many sessions as I can and when you have reached any conclusions or have any recommendations on a future course of action, I will want to hear them immediately," said Stevens as he closed the meeting.

Upon returning to his office John Talbot told his secretary, "Get a hold of Tom Garrison in Dallas and get him on a plane. I want him in my office at 9:00 AM in the morning and see if you can get Ed Gorman on the phone. Track him down if you have to. I want Bill Sisson and Jane Henson in my office at 9:00 AM also. Clear my calendar for the entire morning."

Talbot's secretary buzzed him a few minutes later and said, "I have Ed Gorman on line three."

Talbot picked up the phone and said, "Ed, how are you?"

"I was doing fine until your secretary called. Am I in trouble?" Gorman asked jokingly.

"Nothing like that, Ed, but if you have anything you want to confess, I will be glad to listen. I need your help on something, Ed, and wondered if you could meet me in my office at 8:45 in the morning."

"Only if you promise that I won't be arrested."

"I promise, Ed, unless you do something stupid during the night. I will see you at 8:45."

At 8:45 the next morning Ed Gorman was sitting across from the desk of John Talbot. "Ed, this is going to sound crazy and I must rely on your discretion whether you agree to my proposal or not. I believe that you will be able to appreciate the sensitivity of the subject and will honor my request for complete secrecy now and later, if necessary."

Gorman nodded and Talbot began to outline the events of the recent past down to the formation of the special task force and his request that Gorman serve.

"Why would you want me on an investigative task force?"

"Ed, if our theory is correct you will be able to bring a political perspective to the table that none of the rest of us have, and that could be very important."

"Okay, if you think I can help," replied Gorman.

"Good. Now we are going into the next room and you can meet your fellow task force members," said Talbot as he strode across the room and opened the door to the adjoining conference room.

All eyes looked up as Talbot and Gorman entered the room.

"Folks, so glad that you could make it on such short notice. This is Ed Gorman and although he is an outsider he will be assisting us in this endeavor. Deborah, I think you know Ed but the rest of you go around the table and tell Ed who you are and what you do for a living."

After the introductions all around Talbot gave the group a briefing on recent events and told them what they would be doing.

"We are going to operate on the assumption, albeit, merely a theory, that there is a conspiracy in motion to eliminate persons whom someone or some group thinks are extremists. We've never encountered anything like this on this scale so we are going to have to think outside the box: No idea, no matter how far out it may be is to be discounted. We will need to fully air all our thoughts and see if we can come up with answers or, at least, something that will steer us in the right direction. Assuming that the Attorney General can make it we're going to begin our sessions on Monday morning, 9:00 AM in this room. Unless you are contacted and told otherwise, be here then. Start your thinking and be ready to go Monday morning. I have files for each of you to study over the weekend and I am sure that I do not have to remind you of the sensitivity of this information and the need to keep it close to the vest. That's it for the day."

When the others had departed, Talbot rang the Attorney Generals' office and when he came on the line he said, "I have the task force ready to go at 9:00 AM Monday morning if that suits you and I think it would be wise to hold the meeting in my personal conference room if you don't mind coming over."

"I will be there and you are right: All those people parading in and out of my quarters might raise a few eyebrows. I will see you Monday morning."

Chapter 18

On Monday morning the Attorney General entered the conference room at FBI Director John Talbot's office. He said hello and shook the hands of all the task force members.

"I understand that you have all been briefed on what this group is about. Let me reiterate the need for secrecy at this point. We have no idea of what or who, if anything, we are dealing with but we feel that what has happened so far stretches the notion of coincidence a little far. We may be wrong and that would please me greatly if we are, but, in the meantime, we are going to put our minds and skills to work and really dig in to this thing. I believe that each of you has been furnished a complete file of all the data we have assembled so far and that you reviewed it over the weekend. My question to you this morning is whether any of you have formed any opinion on what we are dealing with." said Stevens.

Tom Garrison, the Dallas agent was the first to speak. "There's not a lot to work with here. It is going to take a lot of old fashioned field work in each of these cases and it is going to require the complete cooperation of the local jurisdictions. It is almost like we are going to have to start from scratch in every case."

Bill Sisson, the forensics specialist added, "We do not have the first piece of tangible evidence: no witnesses, no shell casings, and no report of any physical evidence of any kind to begin with. Tom is right. We are going to have to start from scratch and, unfortunately, the crime scenes have been trampled over and a lot of time has passed. I will need to visit every site and at least do a walk through."

"Psychologically speaking, said Jane Henson, my first impression is that we are not dealing with loonies here. This is too sophisticated, too professional, to be the work of fringe elements. I believe that we are dealing with either one very smart dude or a cadre of top notch assassins, which then begs the question of their motive. Then there is the question of who is directing this play."

"The original supposition that first peaked your interest is looking much stronger to me and if we assume that the theory of someone or some group trying to eliminate political extremists is correct, you then have your motive and it becomes a question of figuring out how they are accomplishing the objective and who are they using to do it," said Tom Gorman.

"You have all made good points and operating under the assumption that the conspiracy theory is correct and while we are revisiting and reconstructing the crime scenes, we also need to focus on capabilities: who has the expertise, the professionalism, to do this? We will need to compile a listing of potential assassins and once we have done that, we will start looking for a link to who is giving the marching orders. After that it becomes a question of who is paying the bill," stated Talbot.

"I see that the matter is in very capable hands and I am going to have to leave you now. Thank you all for your work and especially you, Mr. Gorman: You actually had a choice," said Stevens as the others laughed.

When the Attorney General had departed, Talbot said, "Okay folks, here is how we're going to get organized and started. Tom, you'll head up the crime scenes investigation. You can pull as many of our people in as you feel are necessary to get it done but I want you to personally visit every site. I will pave the way for you with the head of the local jurisdictions. Bill, I want you to accompany Tom on all the site visits and see if you can turn up anything that may have been missed. Jane, I want you to put together a psychological profile on who may be behind this and Ed, I want you to begin thinking about the same thing. Feel free to consult with Jane as much as needed."

"Remember folks, mum is the word," said Talbot, signaling the end of the meeting.

G. Lee Greer

Chapter 19

Joe Rollins studied the brief file on his next target, Robert "Bob" Simmons. Simmons was a criminal defense attorney with offices in Washington, D.C. and Baltimore. He had a long list of successful defenses of high profile murderers, drug king pins, pornographers and money launderers. If you had the money, he was the go to guy when you got into trouble. His defenses were notable, not on the facts of guilt or innocence, but on Simmons's ability to twist and contort the law to confuse or discredit the prosecution's case and establish a basis for appeal. It had been said that it would not be unusual for a defendant found guilty to live out a natural life while Simmons made his endless appeals.

He was also an insider in the political circles and a big contributor to Washington politicians. He associated himself with self proclaimed social justice committees. In a word, he was a mover and shaker in D.C. and he loved the attention it brought to him. He was good before the camera and knew how to manipulate the media to emphasize his viewpoint.

His home was in Georgetown and his office in downtown D.C., occupying the top two floors of a towering office building which he owned. He commanded a half million dollar retainer before he would even talk with you and he never declined a case if the accused could come up with the retainer.

Joe packed a bag, stored his weapons in a hidden compartment in his SUV, and headed for Washington. Upon arriving he checked in to the same hotel he had used before and headed for Freddie's and his famous cheeseburgers. Freddie recognized him when he entered and greeted him like an old friend. Joe ordered a draft, a cheeseburger with real french fries, and chatted with Freddie for awhile. Afterwards he returned to his hotel room.

The next day, after putting on a disguise of a hairpiece and a mustache, he drove down to the area of Simmons' building, parked the car and walked around, observing the layout of the area and locating the entrance to the parking garage. He then returned to the main entrance of the building, entered, and pretended to read the message board before taking one of the elevators. He exited the elevator one floor below Simmons' floor, walked the hall pretending to be looking for a particular office and then back to the stairway where he entered and walked down to the second floor and exited. He then took another elevator and rode it down to the garage level. The garage was two levels and most of the parking spaces were marked for personal use. He didn't want to be seen walking around in the garage with no seeming purpose so he took the elevator back up and exited the building through the main entrance. He would return again tomorrow.

The next morning, donning his disguise again, Joe walked to a nearby car rental agency and, using his Connecticut identity, rented a car. He drove downtown to Simmons' building and entered the parking garage through a gated but unmanned entrance, took his parking ticket and when the bar rose he entered the garage and began to cruise around slowly looking for a parking slot with Simmons' name. On the second level in the corner he found what he was looking for and nearby was what had to be a private elevator, available by card only. He then returned to the lower level and parked in a spot marked for visitors and took the elevator up to the main level. He needed to let some time elapse before he exited the garage so he left the building and walked around town like a tourist for about an hour. He then returned to the building and took the stairs down to the garage level and exited the garage through a manned station. The attendant hardly looked at him as he took the ticket and money from him and he was quickly on his way.

Back at the hotel, Joe thought through his plan of action. He intended to catch Simmons coming off the elevator and going to his nearby car. To avoid the security cameras, he would not drive his car into the garage but would enter through the main entrance and take the elevator or stairs down. He planned to exit the same way if the timing coincided with the main entrance doorway not being locked down. If the main entrance was not available he would have to exit the garage at the unmanned entrance gate and try to shield himself as much as possible from a clear shot from the security cameras. He would have to return to the building tomorrow and find out what time the main entrance lock down occurred.

He had decided to use a Beretta 22 with a silencer, the assassin's up close preference. A single shot upward at the base of the skull was almost always lethal. A second shot in the temple or between the eyes would seal the deal.

Now it was a matter of timing. He couldn't hang around the garage all day hoping to find Simmons alone and he had no way of determining Simmons' schedule on a daily basis. He had to go with the most likely scenario that would dictate the time and circumstance for successfully encountering Simmons. He decided to see if maybe he could help dictate events.

Joe found a pay phone, looked up the number of Simmon's firm, and dialed the number. When answered he asked to speak with Mr. Robert Simmons. He was put on hold and momentarily another person answered.

"This is Myrna Chavis, Mr. Simmon's secretary. May I inquire who is calling?"

"My name is not important at this point. I need to talk with Mr. Simmons and see if he can help me."

"Do you know what Mr. Simmons' up front financial requirements are?"

"Yeah. I've heard and that is no problem if I think he can help me."

"Would you like for me to make an appointment for you? I can get you in as early as Tuesday, next week."

"No. That's no good. I need to see him as soon as possible. Tonight, or tomorrow at the latest. I am prepared to turn over to him his half million dollar retainer if I am convinced he can help."

"One moment please."

After a brief period, the secretary came back on the line and said, "Can you come to his office at 7:00 o'clock this evening? Mr. Simmons will be out of town for the rest of the week."

"I'll be there."

At 6:45 PM Joe entered the building by the main entrance and went to the elevator. He did not take the elevator up to Simmons' floor, however, but got off the elevator a couple of floors up and when he noted that the hall was empty, he waited for the elevator and took it down to the garage level. He noticed that most of the cars were gone and he quickly walked up to the second level and over to the area where Simmons parked his car. Down about two spaces from Simmon's car slot there was a recessed area which contained a trash dumpster. Joe had determined on his earlier visit that he could stand beside the dumpster next to the column and have a clear line of site to the elevator while being shielded from view of anyone passing by. He figured that he would have to wait for at least thirty minutes to an hour for Simmons to show. Simmons would wait around for awhile for his client to show before giving it up and leaving, but whenever he showed, Joe would be ready.

Joe took out his Beretta, double checked the load, and affixed the silencer. There was not much traffic up in that area of the garage at that time and Joe kept his eyes fixed on the elevator. At 7:15 the elevator door opened and Joe was prepared to move until he noticed that it was two men, neither of them Simmons. They were probably senior partners who also enjoyed the perk of the private elevator. Joe settled back down to wait. A short time later the door opened again but this was a false alarm too. This time it was a woman, probably a senior partner or an executive secretary.

At 7:45 Joe was wondering if Simmons was going to show at all when the elevator door opened and Simmons headed toward his car. Joe quickly, but not hurriedly, began walking towards him, not looking at or seeming interested in him. Just as Joe walked past him Simmons reached to open his car door and Joe whirled and stepped forward to within three feet of Simmons and pulled the trigger. The bullet entered at the base of the skull and Simmons slumped against the car and then to the floor. He fell onto his back and his open eyes were staring up at him but Joe knew he was dead. He did take the time to put another round between his eyes.

Joe quickly removed the silencer and stuck the gun and the silencer into his coat pockets and made his way down to the lower garage level. He took the elevator up to the main level and exited the building through the main entrance. He had checked out of his room earlier in the day so he made his way across town to turn in his rental car. After doing so and retrieving his own car, he hit I-95 heading south.

A security guard would find the body about an hour later and call the police.

Chapter 20

FBI Director John Talbot was still in his office when he received a phone call advising him of the shooting of Bob Simmons. He got in touch with his assistant and told him to get Tom Garrison and Bill Sisson over to the site, even though they had no jurisdiction, and to get in touch with him, no matter the hour, when they had analyzed the scene. He told him to assure the locals that they were not assuming jurisdiction but merely wanted to observe what they were looking at.

Talbot phoned the Attorney General at home and advised him of Simmons' death.

"Okay, John. Start another file and add it to the pot. I will advise the President."

When the President answered the Attorney General's call he began by saying, "Edmund, I'm beginning to dread your phone calls."

"No more so than I dread making them, Mr. President, answered the Attorney General, and I'm afraid that I have some more bad news. Bob Simmons was shot and killed tonight and we think he fits the profile."

"Damn, Edmund, where does this end?"

"I don't know, Mr. President, but I think that you and I need to put our heads together tomorrow before my press conference on Wednesday and yours on Thursday so that I can bring you up to speed and make sure that we are singing off the same page."

"You're right, Edmund. I'll have someone call you in the morning, said the President as he signed off.

The news broke fast and furious and the media feeding frenzy began. It came with a report on one of the networks evening news when one of the field reporters recounted the information of the deaths of recent past and the now known fact that they were execution style slayings, followed by the open question as to whether these slayings might be interrelated. The anchor posed the question to one of the expert guests who had been brought in and he was quick to offer his opinion, which when said and done meant maybe yes, maybe no."

One of the talking heads spoke, saying, "Look, we have a federal judge, a United States Senator, a Congressman, a Hollywood producer whose claim to fame is pornography, a civil rights activist, though he didn't have much credibility, a noted criminal defense lawyer, and an environmental activist slain, execution style, and it makes you wonder since they were all what might be described as extreme left wingers. Additionally, you have the killing of Charles Dunning, though he doesn't fit the complete profile as the others: he was as far right as they were left. If you include him you could say that this was the work of an equal opportunity assassin or assassins."

Another of the guests chimed in with, "The big question, if the story pans out, is who is behind this. It doesn't seem reasonable to believe that there is a single assassin if you look at the time frames and logistics of the slayings, so there would have to be some small group closely coordinating their efforts or someone giving marching orders. That's a scary picture."

Another quest analyst asked, "Has the Justice Department gotten involved with this or are they as surprised and shocked as we are? I understand that the Attorney General will be holding a news conference in the next couple of days and I'm sure that questions will come up during the President's scheduled press conference on Thursday."

The next day the other networks and all the cable channels picked up on the story and their talking heads were off and running with all kinds of dire predictions and the big question became: Will there be more of these assassinations and the speculation began as to who might be targeted next? One commentator got the attention of the anchor of a major network when he surmised that if the conspirators were targeting what they considered to be left wing extremists and those who trumpeted their line they might even go after a major newscaster. When he saw the eyes of the news anchor widen and his face begin to pale, he regretted having made such a suggestion and started backpedaling but the thought had been registered. He would not be invited back again.

One Congressman took to the floor of the House and, after railing against the extreme right wing and their evil ways, called on the administration to immediately provide 24 hour protection for all the members of Congress and all federal judges. When it was pointed out to him that this would require more manpower than was presently employed as agents of the FBI, the Secret Service, and the United States Marshall's Service combined he would not be dissuaded and said that, if necessary, they could use the armed forces.

The call in talk shows all across the country were having a field day too. They couldn't talk about anything else. There were the usual nut cases ranting both pro and con but there was developing a calm, thoughtful undercurrent of opinion that while the killings were to be condemned in the strongest possible terms, maybe there was a rationale, whether you agreed with it or not, to what was going on. Maybe things had reached a point in this country where people were just fed up with the direction we were going, against the will and desire of the vast majority, but being orchestrated by politicians and judges. If the politicians were expecting an overwhelming reaction against the killings, they were sorely disappointed and as politicians do, once they gauged the wind, they began to tone down their rhetoric.

The President called in the senate majority and minority leaders, the Speaker of the House and ranking minority member and the Attorney General for a meeting in his office.

"Gentlemen, we may have a situation on our hands. As you are aware, now that the story has broken, there are a lot of very edgy people in this town and everybody has their own theory as to what is going on. What we don't need is to make the situation worse by wild ranting and ravings of our elected officials. We must stay calm and use our influence to calm the others. There will be those who will try to make political hay out of this but this is too serious to let them rule the day. We will need to be prepared to offer calming comments every time one of them opens their mouth," said the President.

"That's all well and good, Mr. President, but we're going to have to be able to provide some answers and reassurances to our colleagues and the American people and we are completely in the dark on this," offered the majority leader with a little edge in his voice.

"I appreciate that and the Attorney General is going to brief you now on where we are but there is not a hell of a lot he or anyone else can tell you at this point," answered the President.

"We first hit on the possibility of a correlation of these killings a couple of weeks ago. At that time there were five deaths that we thought fit the profile. Since then there have been three more. We have assembled a special task force to look into this and FBI Director John Talbot is personally heading it up. They are just getting started and there is literally nothing that we can tell you at this point other than that we think, and the operative work here is think, that a conspiracy exists to eliminate certain political extremists. It is going to take some time to thoroughly investigate these eight killings and try to reach some conclusions which will point us in the right direction as to who may be responsible for this. I realize that you are going to be under pressure from the media just as we are, but I'm asking you to be patient until we can come up with something. At this point we have not a shred of evidence to go on and it is a theoretical exercise until we can hit on something," said the Attorney General.

"What about protection?" asked the Speaker of the House?

"For whom?" posed the Attorney General.

"At a minimum, for the political leadership and possibly for the members of the Supreme Court."

"We are prepared to do that but we can't go any further than that unless we have a credible threat against someone. We simply don't have the manpower to cover everyone as has been suggested by one of the House members," answered the Attorney General.

"And this protection will be put in place without fanfare or announcement. It will just be there starting this evening and we are asking you to not speak of it for if you do you are going to have to explain to your colleagues and the public why you have protection and they don't," interjected the President.

The Attorney General continued, "We plan to brief you on a weekly basis and more often if there are significant developments. In the meantime, we ask you for your patience and we will try to give you as much political cover as possible."

"Are there any questions or comments any of you may have?" asked the President.

Everyone looked at each other but none spoke and the President said, "Thank you, gentlemen. We will keep you posted."

Chapter 21

In his office, Peck pulled out his special phone and keyed in speed dial two. There was no immediate answer but the clicking sound told him that the party had received the call and would make himself available in thirty minutes. When he redialed thirty minutes later the answer came immediately.

"I don't have anything to offer this morning but I wanted to know what you thought of the idea of getting together again and discussing our situation to date and the possibility of further moves." said Peck.

"I think that's a good idea. Would you like for me to set it up the same as last time?" came the answer.

"That would be good. Just let me know," said Peck and he disconnected.

The call came two days later and the message was, "Saturday afternoon, three o'clock, my boat."

"I will see you there," replied Peck.

On Saturday afternoon, once everyone was aboard and they were cruising around Chesapeake Bay, the three of them were ensconced in the forward lounge, which had been electronically swept for listening devices earlier: you couldn't be too careful.

"Well, Gentlemen, what are your feelings on what has transpired so far and your thoughts on further actions from this point forward," said Peck.

"If you lay aside the media frenzy and the dime a dozen big mouths who are screaming Armageddon, there seems to be a sober undercurrent going through this town that I have never seen. After the predictable initial reaction of feigned outrage and political posturing by the demagogues there seems to be a quiet, reflective mood among most people. One of the more liberal congressmen from California was overheard saying that maybe they had taken it too far and that a backlash may be starting. I also have it on pretty good authority that the ranking majority member on the senate judiciary committee, who is in line to assume the chairmanship with the death of Senator Spenser is having second thoughts on whether he wants the job. He has scheduled a news conference for Monday morning to announce his plans: I believe that he is going to decline the chairmanship of judiciary and will give as his excuse that he wants to devote all of his time and energy to banking and finance regulation and that he would have to relinquish his chairmanship of that committee if he accepted the judiciary role. I think that what it really is, is that he is scared shitless about being out front as the spokesman for the far left extremists," said one of the participants.

"Yeah, I have heard the same thing but you know what has amazed me about this whole thing is the lack of righteous indignation and hysteria on the part of the public. The call in show hosts are trying to keep the pot boiling but, by and large, the public has been very calm and in some cases a few have said that it was bound to happen, sooner or later, and maybe now is the time before things get even more out of hand. Never underestimate the American people and their pragmatic view of things. This attitude has concerned the left wing extremists even more than the killings," said the other.

"The question is whether it will have any long term effect, offered Peck, or will it just be business as usual after a cooling off period. Which brings me to the next question: do we need to go forward with more candidates at this time or sit quietly?"

"I think that we need to cool it for awhile and give this thing time to work. There is going to be a massive, all out investigation and we probably don't need to have any of our people active until it blows over. I just hope that these people have covered their tracks well because the justice department is going to go all out on this thing," said one of the others.

"I agree. Let's let it sink in and avoid going any further unless we see that it is absolutely necessary," said the other.

"Okay, said Peck, we are agreed to shut down for awhile."

"Good. Now how about some of my famous Maryland crab cakes and other seafood delicacies which have been prepared for us," said the host.

There was a flurry of news conferences during the next few days, the first being that of the Attorney General. He opened with a statement outlining what had transpired to date and advised the media of the special task force. He tried hard to drive home the point that they were flying blind at this point since they had no evidence of a conspiracy or any clue as to who the perpetrators were.

The first question came. "Mr. Attorney General, is the justice department assuming jurisdiction in these cases?"

"No. At this point, except in the case of Judge Hammond, we have no legal basis to assume jurisdiction nor do we want to. We will, however, be working closely with the local jurisdictions and lending any assistance we can to them. We have talked with all the local jurisdictions and we have agreed to share all the information anyone gathers. If, at some point in time, we develop any evidence that a conspiracy exists we will move to gain joint jurisdiction under the applicable statutes of civil rights violations."

"Sir, are you convinced that the killing of Charles Dunning is a part of this thing? He was not exactly left wing as were the others," asked another reporter.

"We're dealing with perception here, folks. Charles Dunning was not a left winger. He was about as far right as they come but he was perceived, like all the others, to be in the extreme. Until we develop evidence to the contrary we are going to assume that he was an intended target like the others," answered the Attorney General.

"Sir, when was the President made aware of all this?"

"As soon as we at justice developed the theory that these killings might be interrelated, I personally briefed the President on our position and he concurred with our plan to pursue the question. He has been updated on a regular basis, as needed."

"Why was the media and the public not advised earlier of what you were doing?" asked another reporter.

"Look folks, this entire thing is hardly two weeks old and it unfolded slowly. It was only when one of our people developed the theory of a possible conspiracy, did we do anything at all. That was about a week ago. Since then there have been four additional killings and we have in place a special task force to look at it. By Washington standards, that is moving pretty quickly. I must reiterate and stress to you that we are still dealing in theory and do not have any evidence as to the killer or killers or whether there is in fact a conspiracy. Until we develop some hard evidence it does no good to speculate any further," said the Attorney General.

The press conference ended on that note even though the media hounds wanted to hear more than speculation. They wanted to start the blame game.

The President's news conference went pretty much the same except he did not address the question in his opening statement. His answers mimicked those given by the Attorney General as there was very little that he could add to the subject. The question of protection did come up and the Presidents response was that that matter would be dealt with as needed but would not be addressed publicly.

On Monday Morning at ten o'clock there was a news conference held in the senate judiciary committee hearing room. Present were the majority leader, Senator Ed Jennings, the ranking majority member and Senator William Hartley, the second ranking majority member.

The majority leader opened the news conference with a statement, "The Senate is saddened by the death of Senator Cabot Spenser, the former chairman of the Senate Judiciary Committee. His leadership of the committee and his personal counsel and camaraderie will be sorely missed by all who knew and respected him. Unfortunately, the business of the Senate and this great nation must go on so we must cut short and lay aside our personal sense of loss and get on with what we have been sent here to do. This morning I have here with me two of the most distinguished members of the Senate. First, there is Senator Ed Jennings, the ranking majority member of the committee. At this time, he will make a brief statement."

"Ladies and gentlemen, as the ranking majority member of the Senate Judiciary Committee I was in line and, in fact, was offered the Chairmanship of Judiciary. I have respectfully declined the chairmanship for the following reason. As you know I am currently the Chairman of the Senate Finance Committee and that is where I want to concentrate my efforts. I would have to give up that chair in order to fill the other and I decline to do so and in fairness to my colleague who will be accepting the chairmanship I have today submitted my resignation from the Judiciary Committee altogether." With these comments Senator Jennings stepped back and the majority leader stepped forward again.

"If you will, hold your questions until all the statements have been made. At this time I would like to introduce the new

Chairman of the Senate Judiciary Committee, Senator William Hartley, who will make a brief statement."

"Ladies and gentlemen, I am pleased and am thankful to my colleagues for the honor and confidence they have shown me. I can think of no greater service or responsibility than serving as Chairman of the Judiciary Committee. I pledge to give it my best effort."

The majority leader stepped forward again and opened the conference for questions.

"Senator Jennings, it has been suggested that you would like to have remained on Judiciary but that you did not relish the idea of being out front as the spokesman for the left wing, which would have been expected of you. Would you care to comment on that?" asked the reporter.

"I have given my reasons for doing what I am doing and the suggestion that I am shying away from an active role in my party is baseless and without merit," replied the Senator.

"Senator Hartley, do you intend to run the committee the same way as your predecessor who was viewed by many as an obstructionist who would block, at all costs, any nominee who would not tow the liberal line?" asked another reporter.

"I will be issuing a statement in the near future, after I have had a chance to meet with the members of the committee, which will state clearly the rules under which we will operate," replied Senator Hartley.

That drew a puzzled glance from the majority leader and Senator Jennings. Apparently the new chairman had not been given his marching orders yet or he had misunderstood what was expected of him.

"Sir, do you think the death of Senator Spenser was attributable in any way to his conduct as chairman of Judiciary? He was clearly viewed as an obstructionist to the fair and timely hearing of any judicial nominee with whom he had a difference of ideological opinion."

The majority leader stepped forward and responded, "I would hate to think that he was killed because of his political views and how he applied them. He was a freely elected member of this body who was sent here by his constituents to act on their behalf. It is frightening to think that one's political views, no matter the viewpoint, is a justification for murder. I would also hate to think that the duly elected members of the Congress are capable of being intimidated by anyone who has a different viewpoint."

"But Sir, he clearly was out of step with the full senate as witnessed by the numerous occasions when they forced the question on judicial nominees whom he had refused to report out of committee. Do you see this policy continuing?"

"Senator Hartley has stated that he will announce the rules under which the committee will operate in the coming days. Let's hold off on any judgments until then," said the majority leader and with that he concluded the news conference.

Chapter 22

It had been two weeks since the special task force had begun its work and they were now assembled in the FBI Director's conference room for their first review.

"All right, folks, let's see where we are," said Talbot.

"I guess I can start, said Garrison. Bill and I have visited all of the crime scenes and talked with the locals. We have seen everything that they have, which isn't much. All that I can state with any authority is that these were all professional hits by some very good people of their trade and, quite frankly, we still haven't come across any evidence that would point us in the right direction."

"I concur in what Tom has said and would add that I have never encountered cases that were so void of physical evidence and or witnesses. These were real pros," said Sisson.

"Jane or Ed, have either of you been able to come up with anything yet?" asked Talbot.

"I can give you a thumbnail sketch of what I think at this point, said Henson. The person or persons are well educated and prosperous. They love their country and in their minds they are very concerned with the direction this country is going. They are also very knowledgeable about the government and the players in this town and across the country. They are trying to send a message; a message of intimidation and notice: That they are fed up and are not going to take it any more. They are willing to expend large sums of money to achieve their ends. They believe that they can get by with it just by being smarter and very careful. It is highly unlikely that the people doing the killing have the remotest idea who they are working for. They are in it for the money and are being paid very well."

"That's a hell of a sketch, Jane. Ed, can you add anything to what Jane has said or do you have a different viewpoint?" asked Talbot.

"I concur with Jane's assessment. We have talked a good bit and keep coming back to one strong point. This person or persons is trying to send a message to the political extremists, particularly those who they feel are abusing their power and violating the sense of the large majority of the people in this country. They see no relief coming from the Congress or the courts and they are willing to lay it on the line to at least get some of these people thinking about what they are doing and getting others to think about what they are allowing this small minority of extremists to do by acquiescing or compromising too much for political expediency," said Gorman.

"We have compiled a short list of persons who we think may have knowledge of the players who may engage in the assassination trade and are developing a list of persons with whom we will want to talk. Of course, it would be helpful if we could come up with at least one name we could tie to any of these killings and then work backward from there. Even if we come up with a strong suspect we are no closer to the people who are behind this unless we can apply some extraordinary pressure to gain their cooperation but if these are true professionals, as we all seem to think they are, we cannot anticipate a lot of cooperation," said Talbot.

Tom Garrison interjected, "We have one potential lead on one of the hits. In the case of Lincoln Johnson we have found that a character, not known to any of the locals, showed up in the neighborhood a few days prior to the killing and has not been seen again since the killing. We have a sketch artist working with a local real estate agent and we will be pursuing that. As soon as we have developed our list of potential assassination tradesmen, I will want to compare the sketch with them."

"Does anyone else have anything else to add?" queried Talbot.

There was no response and Talbot closed the meeting with, "We will reconvene here one week from today, same time. Let's hope that we have something to talk about by then."

G. Lee Greer

Chapter 23

Jack O'Neal was interrupted by his secretary who said, "Mr. O'Neal, I have FBI Director John Talbot on line one."

Jack answered the phone with, "Hello, John, it's been awhile since we've talked. What can I do for you?"

"Jack, it's good to talk to you. I need to have some of my people talk to you at your earliest convenience. We are very busy on this conspiracy thing which I am sure you have been reading about and we are trying to develop a list of potential professional hit men around the country and knowing that you have some knowledge of some of the people employed in ops of one kind or another, I was hoping that you might be able to give us some names of people we could look at," said Talbot.

"That's a hell of a request, John. The people that I contract with work mostly off shore for governments or international concerns and deal almost exclusively in security matters. As a matter of fact, a good bit of the work is requested by the good old

USA. I am reluctant to involve these people in this mess," replied O'Neal.

"I understand, Jack, and we are not looking to create any problems for these people and I am not suggesting that any of the people that you may have contracted with in the past has anything to do with our current situation but we need to look at anyone who has the capabilities to pull this kind of thing off and then we will decide if any of them may be inclined to engage in this type of work. We are asking the same thing of some of your competitors, so don't feel like we are picking on you," said Talbot.

"Okay. Send them around about two this afternoon and I will be giving it some thought but I want to stress to you that I don't want any of the names that I may give you put in an awkward position or be exposed to publicity. Are we agreed?" asked O'Neal.

"Agreed."

When O'Neal hung up he mused to himself that he needed to maintain a cordial relationship with the FBI Director because he may need a favor somewhere down the road plus he would need to divert attention away from his people. He would pretend to cooperate. "Yeah, right, he muttered to himself, I'll give you some names. Good luck."

At two o'clock, his secretary rang him and said, "Sir, agents Bradford and Wilson are here to see you. They said you were expecting them."

"Send them in, please."

After introductions and small talk, agent Bradford said, "Sir, I believe that the Director told you the purpose of our visit. If we could get the names that you feel may fit the profile we will get out of your way."

JUSTICE REGAINED

"Okay. Bear in mind that the names I am going to give you are persons who possess the capabilities you are looking for and who may or may not be willing to engage in this type work. They have worked for me at one time or another, mostly off shore and mostly in jobs that did not entail this type of activity. The first one is a guy named Jeff Waters. I haven't used him for years and the last address I have on him is New Orleans. The next guy is Ian Lambert from right here in Washington or northern Virginia. Another is Brad Sellers from Miami and the final one is named Joe Massaroni from Detroit. Their last known addresses are on this paper. I hope that this is of some help to you and I would reiterate the message that I gave to the Director that you be very discreet in the use of this information. If word got out that I had given you these names my name would be Mudd in this business and I can't afford that."

"Thank you for your time and the information. I can assure you that we will use the information with the utmost discretion," said agent Bradford as they shook hands and departed the office.

Director Talbot called Tom Garrison into his office and said, "Tom, here are the names of thirteen people that we have secured from our sources who could be described as potential perps. We have also included photographs and as much bio as we have on them, mostly from military records. Get our people busy on these, checking their movements during the killing time frames and see if you can whittle the list down to one or more who

may need further scrutiny. Get back to me as soon as you have anything."
"We're on it."

Chapter 24

Peck's intercom rang. It was Helen, his right hand, who said, "Sir, there's a Mr. Fred DuBard on line three who wishes to speak with you. He says that he is the executive producer of Nations Watch, a talk show on one of the networks which airs every Sunday.

"Okay. Thanks, Helen. I'll speak to him."

"Hello, Mr. DuBard. This is Peck Reynolds. What can I do for you?"

"Hello, Mr. Reynolds. I will get right to the point. I would like for you to appear as one of our panelists on the program this Sunday. We will be broadcasting from our Washington studio."

"A couple of questions. What is the topic? Who else is going to be on the panel and why in the world would you want me?"

"The entire one hour is going to be devoted to the recent rash of killings and the theory that a conspiracy exists. The other panelists are the Attorney General and Senator William Hartley, the newly appointed chairman of the Senate Judiciary Committee."

"But why me? I don't fit in with those people."

"You have a reputation, sir. A reputation for candor, a reputation for ethical behavior in all your dealings, you have served on the inside in Washington and are known to be very knowledgeable about how this town works and who the players are. We also know that you are not the most popular figure among those on the hill, particularly the United States Senate, after your dressing down of Senator Folsom. At the same time you are an outsider and I believe that you would lend a different perspective to the discussion."

"You are very persuasive, Mr. DuBard. I am probably a fool for agreeing to do this but I will participate. When and where do you want me?"

"Great, Mr. Reynolds. Be at our Washington studio on Sunday morning at nine thirty. We will tape at ten thirty and the program will air at noon. I look forward to meeting you."

Peck immediately rang Vincent and said, "Vincent, I need to be in Washington on Sunday and I thought I would go down to the farm on Friday. If you are free, I would like for you to go with me. We'll be back on Monday."

"Sounds good to me, boss. What time should I have Gil have the plane ready?" asked Vincent.

"About five o'clock."

Peck sat at his desk and thought of Mary Leigh Braxton and the idea that this might be a good opportunity to invite her down to his place which he had been promising to do for years. He thumbed through his directory, found her number and dialed.

"Hello."

"Mary Leigh, don't faint dead away but this is Peck and I am calling to invite you down to the farm for the weekend; this weekend. I know that it is short notice and you are probably committed but the trip just came up and I thought of you. Any chance you can make it?"

"Well, Peck, let me catch my breath. Of course, I will come. When are you arriving?"

"Vincent and I will get there on Friday afternoon around six thirty. You can drive down or if you prefer, I can send Vincent up to drive you down Friday evening or Saturday morning. By the way, I have a little commitment mid day on Sunday but the rest of the time we can just relax. I have a pretty good cook down there and if it is all right with you, we will just plan to eat all our meals there rather than go out."

"I'll plan to drive down on Friday afternoon and will probably get there about the same time as you and eating in sounds great to me. I have had more than enough of dining out lately. I can't believe that you called and I am looking forward to the weekend. I will see you Friday evening. Goodbye, Peck."

Peck rang Vincent again and said," I have invited Mary Leigh Braxton to join us at the farm for the weekend. Call down there and tell them we will be having extra company and that she will be arriving Friday evening."

"That's great, boss. I like Mrs. Braxton. Are you sure that you want me tagging along on this trip?"

"Yes, Vincent. You will be our chaperone."

"Okay, boss, but you must understand that in my role of chaperone I will insist upon the most modest decorum on both your parts."

"Goodbye, Vincent," said Peck as he chuckled.

When they arrived at the farm on Friday evening Mary Leigh was already there. They found her in the kitchen having coffee with Sam and Martha Briggs, the live-in couple who looked after the place for Peck.

Peck gave Mary Leigh a hug and a light peck on the cheek and said, "I see that you have met the folks who run the place."

"Hello Peck. Hello Vincent. It's good to see you again. Peck, I haven't seen much of the place but it is beautiful down here. I am looking forward to a full guided tour."

"And you shall have it. I'm going to shower and change into my farm clothes, jeans and a sweatshirt, for the rest of the evening. Mary Leigh, please feel free to dress comfortably and very informal. Why don't we meet back in the den in about an hour for drinks and then we'll have dinner about eight, if that suits you," said Peck.

"Martha, I do not know what you have prepared but you will be feeding a lady who has eaten high on the hog all over the world, but don't feel intimidated. She's just a down home girl from South Carolina," joked Peck.

"Mr. Reynolds, I have put Mrs. Braxton in the bedroom suite by the pool, if that is all right. I will be ready to serve dinner around eight. Just let me know," advised Martha.

"That's fine Martha. A good choice. Now if everyone will excuse me, I will see you all in about an hour," said Peck as he left the room.

Around seven, Peck, Vincent, and Mary Leigh were in the very spacious and comfortable den. Vincent was behind the bar fixing drinks. Mrs. Briggs had laid out some hors d'oeuvres and they were being attacked rather vigorously by all three.

"Peck, I am looking forward to a full tour of the place tomorrow and the entire weekend just doing nothing," said Mary Leigh. She had taken her cue from Peck and was dressed casually in jeans and a baggy sweater.

"Mary Leigh, I am delighted that you were able to come down and I apologize again for the short notice but I did not know we were coming down until about five minutes before I called you. I have been invited to appear on Nations Watch on Sunday morning in the Washington studio and that will take about four hours total. Except for that I am devoted to your desires and comfort for the full weekend."

"That's exciting, Peck. What is the program about that would lure you into such public exposure? I know how much you have shied away from the limelight."

"It is about the recent killings of some high profile people around the country and the inevitable conspiracy theory. The Attorney General and Senator Hartley will round out the panel. Mr. DuBard, the producer, said that they were looking for a non-political perspective and I am it."

"Peck, if I won't be in the way, I would love to tag along with you and observe. I know these people, of course, but I have never been inside a television studio. I would like to see how it is done and the subject intrigues me."

"That's great, Mary Leigh. You are officially invited. It will be comforting to have another friend nearby to console me if I make a fool of myself."

Mrs. Briggs interrupted to announce that dinner was ready and they adjourned to the dining room. The dinner was superb; stuffed quail with wild rice, a cornbread dressing, a squash casserole and cranberries. After dessert and Mary Leigh's good hearted attempt to lure the Briggs's away from Peck and to come to work for her they returned to the den for after dinner drinks.

After finishing his brandy, Peck said, "I'm going to have to walk off some of that great dinner I just consumed. Mary Leigh, Vincent, would ya'll like to take a stroll with me?"

Mary Leigh quickly assented but Vincent feigned the desire to stay and watch something on television so that Peck and Mary Leigh could have some time alone. As they exited the rear of the house, Mary Leigh wrapped her arm in Peck's and they strolled a partially lit path about two hundred yards back to the main horse barn. The barn was lit with subdued lighting and upon entering the barn Peck threw a switch which fully lit up the place. It was an impressive structure; stalls for sixteen horses, a tack room, a vet's treatment room, an office, a lounge room, a workshop, two wash stalls, and a feed room. The loft spaces could store enough hay to last for months. Most of the stalls were occupied with beautiful thoroughbred stock.

"Peck, this is most impressive but I didn't know you were a horse farmer," said Mary Leigh.

"I'm not. None of these belong to me. When I bought the place I struck a deal with a couple of my neighbors and in return for using the place they look after the barns and pastures. Without doing any work or spending any money I get to stand around and admire the place. I strongly recommend such an arrangement if you ever decide to own such a place."

"I will keep that in mind. I have been thinking lately that I have about had it with the D.C. scene and that I might buy a place like this or possibly even move back home to Charleston. I miss the quiet pace of things down home and my old friends and relatives."

"It's strange that you should say that because that is exactly what I have been thinking. When I was visiting mother a few weeks ago I promised her that she would be seeing a lot more of me. I said that without thinking and with no plans but I think internally I have made up my mind to abandon the race and just go home and relax but if I do I am not sure that I will want to get rid of this place. It has sort of grown on me and I dearly love spending time here."

Mary Leigh squeezed his arm and Peck felt her breast pressing on his arm and a tinge of excitement ran through him that he had not felt in a long time. He was like a high school kid again. He didn't know what to say or do. It was as if his feet were nailed to the floor. Mary Leigh sensed his uneasiness and she extricated her arm from him and walked over and threw the main switch which Peck had turned on when they entered the barn. The barn returned to the subdued lighting and she turned and walked back to Peck and stood in front of him. When he didn't move she reached out and took his hands and placed his arms around her waist and said, "Kiss me, Peck."

Peck, without speaking, slowly moved to her and gently pressed his lips against her slightly parted lips. It was a gentle kiss, not deeply passionate, not moving, but Peck didn't want it to end. Mary Leigh did not force it either and they just stood there, content to be in each others arms with their lips gently touching. Peck broke off the kiss but he did not leave the embrace; he just stood there looking into her eyes.

"I have to tell you, Peck, that I have wanted that to happen for a long time, and I am not ashamed to admit it," said Mary Leigh.

"I guess that I have felt the same way but was not willing to admit it to myself. Since Phyllis passed away I guess that I have put my emotions on hold and not allowed anything or anyone to penetrate my thoughts. I am glad that it happened and it could only have happened with you," responded Peck.

They closed again and this time the kiss was more passionate but it was just the kiss. There was no groping, but just two people who had finally found each other. They broke the kiss quietly, as if on cue and turned together and walked from the barn and back to the house. At the house, Peck walked Mary Leigh to her room and said, "I will see you in the morning at breakfast." Neither one of them would find it easy getting to sleep.

Chapter 25

Vincent and Peck were in the dining room having coffee when Mary Leigh strode in with a hearty, "Good morning."

"Good morning, Mrs. Braxton," answered Vincent.

"Good morning, Mary Leigh," said Peck.

"Vincent, you need to call me Mary Leigh. You are making me feel like some kind of grand matron."

"Yes, maam."

"And drop the maam too. It's just Mary Leigh."

Mrs. Briggs entered the room with the question, "What would everyone like for breakfast? We have any kind of eggs you want, lean slab bacon, sausage, grits, hash rounds, sweet rolls, toast, and cereal and fruits."

"My heavens, Mrs. Briggs, if you keep this up, I will have to buy a new wardrobe before I leave the place. I usually just have toast, juice, and coffee in the mornings," said Mary Leigh.

"We always eat a hearty breakfast around here, don't we Vincent?" said Peck.

"Yes sir. I dream about Mrs. Briggs's breakfast at night and wake up with great anticipation," replied Vincent.

"Well, just tell me how you want your eggs. The rest will be on platters and in bowls and you can take what you like," advised Mrs. Briggs.

They all gave their egg orders and Mrs. Griggs ambled off to the kitchen.

"Mary Leigh, let me tell you about the day I have planned for us. Nothing is structured and we can deviate or eliminate any part or all of the plan if we decide. After breakfast, I thought we would get in our leg work after the big meal and look at the barns again and the surrounding buildings. Then we'll take the truck and ride the perimeter of the property and the pastures. The horses should be turned out and running around. Then we'll ride down to the pond. It's about a six acre pond and there is a guest house down there. We will break for lunch somewhere in there and then move around some more. We will finish up soon enough to get in a little rest before dinner. If this doesn't suit we will do whatever you like," said Peck.

"Sounds like a plan to me," said Mary Leigh.

Breakfast was served and Vincent and Peck dug in with gusto. Mary Leigh started out slowly but she tried a little of everything and was still eating when the others had finished.

When she laid her eating utensils down, she said, "I cannot believe that I have just consumed all the food that I have. I have never, ever, eaten a breakfast like that but it was so delicious. I feel so guilty and sinful but at the same time, so satisfied."

Peck laughed and Vincent wore a big grin on his face. Mary Leigh joined in and laughed with them.

Vincent said, "I am going to join you two for the walk around but after that you are on your own. I plan to lounge around the pool today and catch up on some reading."

"Well, if everyone has had enough breakfast, let's get started," said Peck.

The walking tour lasted about an hour with Mary Leigh asking a lot of questions about everything she saw. Peck was enjoying himself playing guide and host to Mary Leigh. Vincent noticed that Peck had a little extra spring in his step and was unusually talkative and he attributed that to Mary Leigh's presence. Vincent felt good inside seeing his boss and friend behaving like his old self again. After the walking tour, Vincent dropped off back at the house and Peck and Mary Leigh took the pickup truck and began the riding tour. They rode the perimeter roads with Peck pointing out the property lines and things of interest. They then rode back to the pastures; there were three of them about ten acres each with white fencing. Peck stopped the truck and they got out and leaned on the rail of one of the pastures, watching the horses run and enjoying the view. Peck stood with his arms draped across the top rail and Mary Leigh stood closely to him with one arm resting on his.

"Oh Peck, this is such a beautiful place. I don't see how you are able to leave this place and go back to the city. It is so quiet and restful," said Mary Leigh.

"It is that but with you here it's like I am seeing it fresh all over again. You know I bought this place after Phyllis passed away and I guess I never really fully appreciated what I have although I did enjoy coming here. I see it differently now, thanks to you."

"Peck, about last night, I meant what I said and I guess that I am hoping that we can build on that. Like you, I have been lonely since my husband passed away years ago and although I have had a lot of would be suitors I just never was interested in any of them. You are the only man who has occupied my thoughts and I am hoping that you are at a point where we can spend some serious time together at whatever pace you want to go."

"Mary Leigh, I lay in bed last night thinking about what had happened and I realized that that short moment with you changed my life forever. I enjoyed it as much or more than you did and I didn't feel guilty. If it suits you, from this moment forward you're my girl and I'm your guy and we will just see where it leads us."

"Oh, Peck," Mary Leigh said as she embraced Peck and kissed him with all the passion she had. They stood there a long time, saying nothing, just gazing out over the fields, lost in their thoughts of their new found relationship.

They went on to the pond, as Peck called it, though it was really a small lake. There was a cottage near the water and Peck opened it up for Mary Leigh. She walked through every room, not saying anything until she had seen everything and then saying, "It's beautiful. I think I could live here and be perfectly content."

"It is nice. Sometimes I come down here just to sit and read. It is so isolated and quiet."

They left the cottage and made their way back to the house. It was early afternoon and time for lunch. Vincent was sitting at the table in the kitchen eating a sandwich and Peck and Mary Leigh pulled out chairs and joined him.

"I am reluctant to ask since I had made a vow to myself not to eat again until dinner, but what kind of sandwich is that? It smells so good," said Mary Leigh.

"It is sliced pork barbeque with some extra barbeque sauce generously applied."

"Mrs. Briggs, would you be so kind to fix me one of those?" asked Mary Leigh.

"And I'll have the same with some sweet iced tea," said Peck.

"What did I tell you Mrs. Briggs? I knew they wouldn't be able to resist," said Vincent with a big grin.

Mrs. Briggs smiled as she began preparing their lunch. She was enjoying their hearty appetites and their obvious pleasure and appreciation of her efforts.

After lunch, Peck and Mary Leigh decided to forego any further touring and lounged around the pool with Vincent. Dinner was another event and afterward Peck said, "Mary Leigh, there's one other thing I want to show you and its best seen at night. Vincent, you are welcome to come along if you like."

"No thanks. You two enjoy yourselves."

Peck and Mary Leigh piled into the pickup truck and headed out. After a short ride they pulled up in front of the cottage at the pond. As they were alighting from the truck Mary Leigh asked, "Is there something here I didn't see before?"

Peck said nothing and took her hand and led her into the cottage. He turned on the lights in the den, took her hand again, and led her to the bedroom. He did not turn on the light but left the door ajar so that there was indirect light coming from the den.

Peck took her into his arms and said, "You can stop me if you like. Just say so."

Mary Leigh said nothing and pressed her body tightly against his and they kissed long and deep. Afterward, they lay quietly in bed, side by side, holding hands and not saying anything.

After awhile Peck said, "I don't know about you but I thought that was pretty good for people our age."

"It was absolutely wonderful as I knew it would be. It feels so good and so right to be with you. I have been fantasizing about this moment for a long time and the real thing was even better."

They lay there in each others arms knowing that they were beginning a new phase of their lives and happy in their thoughts.

Chapter 26

At breakfast, Vincent noticed the glow in both Peck and Mary Leigh and the looks and smiles darting back and forth between them. He just smiled inwardly and pretended not to notice. After breakfast they made their way into Washington and the television studio. On arriving they were met by Fred DuBard, the producer, and Peck was advised that the Attorney General and Senator Hartley had already arrived and were in make-up.

"Mr. DuBard, I would like to introduce to you Mary Leigh Braxton and my assistant, Vincent Havel. With your permission they would like to stand off camera and observe the goings on. If you will just show them where you want them, I am sure that they will stay out of the way."

"Of course. We're delighted to have both of you. Ms. Braxton, I know of you but have never had the pleasure of meeting you. We have coffee and other refreshments and you are welcome to help yourselves. Mr. Reynolds, you may want to join the other two in makeup and get your nose dusted. You may not think you need it but it does make a difference to the camera."

Peck nodded and followed Mr. DuBard into the makeup room.

"Gentlemen, I believe that you know Mr. Reynolds," said Mr. DuBard.

"Hello, Peck," said the Attorney General.

"Hello, Peck, it's good to see you again," said Senator Hartley.

"Mr. Attorney General, Senator, it is good to see both of you. I hope that you will take pity on a neophyte who is not used to this sort of thing and go easy on me if I seem nervous and possibly incoherent. I am still not sure that I understand what I am doing here and what I can possibly contribute to the subject."

"We are all treading lightly on this one, Peck, since we're still not sure of what we are dealing with. You will be fine and it will be over before you know it. The moderator will try to keep us focused in the direction he will try to take this thing, and I am not sure exactly what that is myself," said the Attorney General.

After everyone was made up to the makeup artist's satisfaction, they were asked to take their places so that the cameras could line up their angles and run their checks. They were joined by Bill Streett, the longtime moderator of the program who chatted casually with everyone as the mike tests were run. The assistant director signaled five minutes and the makeup artist did some last minute touchup on Streett. Mary Leigh and Vincent were directly off camera but in a clear line of view to Peck and he smiled at them both.

The director signaled the moderator that they were live and he began the program with,

"Good morning, gentlemen. We are going to focus our program today on the recent rash of killings of some notable people around the country and the speculation that a conspiracy exists to eliminate persons who are viewed by some as having extreme views, titled to the left on the political spectrum. Our panelists today are Attorney General Edmund Stevens, Senator William Hartley, the newly named chairman of the senate judiciary committee, and Mr. Boone "Peck" Reynolds, a financier and former Secretary of the Treasury."

"Mr. Attorney General, has there been any change or additional information you can share with us since your most recent press conference?" Street asked.

"No, Bill, but we are working hard at what little information we have. The task force is composed of some extremely capable people and they are going to be looking at everything and everybody that might shed some light on the subject. We know that we are looking at some highly sophisticated people who have done a very good job of covering their tracks up to this point. We can't even say for sure that the killings are related or that a conspiracy exists but we are operating of the assumption that it does exist and will continue to do so until something suggests otherwise," answered the Attorney General.

"Senator, it is pretty well known that the late Senator Spenser was an extreme left winger and, as chairman of the senate judiciary committee, an obstructionist who would do anything necessary to keep judicial nominees whose views he did not like off the bench. Is it your intention to run the committee in the same manner or can we look for something different from you?" queried the moderator.

"Bill, I think it is safe to say that you can look for things to be a little different but I am not prepared today to give any specifics because I have not had a chance to meet with the full committee and discuss my ideas and hear their ideas on how we should operate. After we have met and agreed, in principle, on our method of operation, the committee will have a press conference and announce to the nation exactly how we are going to proceed. Hopefully, this can be accomplished by the end of the week. We have a meeting scheduled for Tuesday.

"Mr. Reynolds, you are very familiar with the beltway scene, who the players are, and generally how things get done around here. What do you make of all this and do you think a conspiracy does exist to rid our political process of extremists." asked Streett.

"Whether a conspiracy exists or not the atmosphere gives us pause to reflect on where we are headed as a nation and whether our political leadership is capable or willing to face up to the problem of the few extremists, who are a small but loud minority, setting the agenda and dictating policy. When you couple that with a judiciary that seems intent on substituting their personal judgment based on their feelings rather than constitutional law and then you throw into the mix elected officials who are beholden to special interests and narrow interests, whose mission in life seems to be to be reelected and the public be dammed, I would say that we have a lot to think about and if these current circumstances contribute to that thought then

I guess some good can come from these tragic circumstances," asserted Peck.

The moderator pounced on Peck's statement and asked, "Mr. Attorney General, Senator, is this what we need to be doing, focusing on the atmosphere which may have produced these events or the acts of killing itself?"

"I believe that we need to do both but our first priority must be to find these people who are responsible and put an end to it and then we can reflect on the social and political atmosphere which may have, in the minds of the perpetrators, prompted these tragic events," said the Attorney General.

"I concur with the Attorney General. There is no justification for the killing of a human being for political reasons and I do not believe that things are quite as bad as Mr. Reynolds seems to suggest. The free and open discussion of ideas and viewpoints is essential to a democracy and if we reach a point in this country where persons are intimidated to the point that they might compromise their political beliefs and positions for fear of mortal retribution, we have seen the end of democracy," said Senator Hartley.

"What about that, Mr. Reynolds? Are things as bad as you seem to think they are?" asked the moderator.

"I believe that we are perilously close to a breakdown in this country and the polls would suggest that a large majority of the American people think so too and yet, most of our political leadership rocks merrily along, seemingly oblivious to what is going on because they are focused on the next election, rather than the problems in this country," said Peck.

"Our judiciary issues their opinions from on high often based on a "feel good" mentality rather than law and we are letting them get away with it. You know, Alexander Hamilton, when commenting on the three branches of the newly formed government, said that "the judiciary is the least dangerous branch of the federal government because it has no influence over either the sword or the purse." Well, he couldn't have been more wrong. In my opinion, which I believe is shared by a lot of others, the judiciary is the greatest threat to freedom in this country and no one is challenging them. They render these ridiculous opinions which become law, without debate and without legislative action and which affect us all and we are meekly accepting these incremental erosions of our liberty. When a candidate for judicial appointment is recommended that doesn't jibe with the far lefts' viewpoint, as demonstrated by the former chairman of the Senate Judiciary committee, that appointment is blocked. It is time to challenge these people in the interest of the nation."

"We are going to follow up on these intriguing thoughts after a short commercial break," said the moderator. The director cued everyone that they were off air for three minutes but to please hold their positions.

"Peck, you are laying it on pretty heavy. Do you really think things are as bad as you suggest?" asked the Attorney General.

"Yes, I do and if you guys would get out and talk with people more I believe that you would sense what I do."

"Peck, what do you mean when you say we need to challenge the judiciary?" asked Senator Hartley.

"There are a number of things you can do. You begin by giving all judicial nominees a fair and timely hearing and you send your recommendation to the full senate for an up or down vote. The constitution talks about the "advise and consent of the senate", not the advise and consent of the senate judiciary committee or the advise and consent of the chairman of the committee. You also legislatively challenge some of these outrageous opinions by passing overriding legislation and in the most extreme and egregious cases, you impeach the bastards."

"Gentlemen, fifteen seconds to live," cued the assistant director. Senator Hartley looked pensively at Peck but there was not time to follow up on his comments.

They were back live and the moderator continued with, "Mr. Reynolds, in your earlier comments you referred to the special interests and narrow interests to which the politicians were beholden. Do you think that these interests are directing the flow of things in Washington?" Are our elected officials in the bag, so to speak, of these special interests?"

"Let me begin by saying that over the years I have given tens of thousands of dollars to political candidates and will continue to do so but never, ever, have I asked for political or legislative favoritism as a condition of those contributions. My interest is in good government by people who I think have the best interests of the nation at heart but I know that there is a lot of money being thrown around out there and the motives of some of the donors and some of the recipients are not so pure. They expect something for their investment and they have been getting it in a lot of cases. We hear a lot of noise about the need for campaign finance reform because the system is being corrupted by all this money. I submit to you that there is no such thing as a corrupt system; there are only corrupt people. We do not need campaign finance reform: all we need is honorable people. If you have honorable people, corruption is not possible."

"Are you saying, Mr. Reynolds, that we don't have honorable people serving in Washington?" asked the moderator.

"Everyone will have to be their own judge as to who is honorable and who is not. I know some elected officials in this town who I consider honorable. I just wish there were more of them."

"Senator, Mr. Reynolds has raised some interesting points which may have some bearing on the motivation of the conspirators, if they exist at all. Do you have any comment to make on his rather frank assertions?" asked the moderator.

"Mr. Reynolds is famous for his frank assertions. That is one of the reasons he is so respected by some and disliked by others in this town and I am going to think long and hard about what he said and I am going to talk with and listen to a lot of people over the next few weeks. To the point Mr. Reynolds made about the judiciary, and more specifically about some of our judges, I do think we are going to have to reflect more on what we are looking for in a judge and I do think that nominees deserve a fair hearing, whether you support them or not.

The program continued awhile in much the same vain and when it was concluded Attorney General Edmund Stevens said, "Peck, you didn't do too badly for a neophyte and I appreciate your comments although I don't necessarily agree with your assessment of some things. I've got to run and do another of these things. Good to see you."

Senator Hartley shook Peck's hand and said, "Peck, I would like to continue our conversation sometime. You have given me some things to think about. I will call you in a few days to see if we can get together. I enjoyed being with you."

Fred DuBard came over to Peck and taking his hand said, "I had a feeling that I made a good call when I asked you to be on the program. Our switchboard is lit up like a Christmas tree and the comments are running about ten to one favorable. I may want you back again in the near future. You are good for business."

"Don't count on that. I am glad that I was able to do this one time but I have no intention of turning into a "talking head." "Now, if you will excuse me I need to get back out to the farm," said Peck as he shook Mr. DuBard's hand.

Peck made his way over to Mary Leigh and Vincent and they were grinning from ear to ear.

"A star is born. Peck, you were wonderful. And so eloquent," said Mary Leigh.

"Great job, boss. You really nailed it," added Vincent.

"Thank you. Now let's get out of here and head back to the farm."

As they rode back to the farm, Peck reflected on the program and what he had said. "You know, it was amazing. Once the program started, I forgot all about the cameras and microphones. It was like I was sitting in my den having a spirited discussion with friends.

The time just flew by. I don't remember half of what I said. I just hope I didn't come across as overbearing or preachy."

"Believe me, Peck, you came across really well and your message was firm and clear. The public is not used to that sort of candor and I am sure that it was well received. You're my hero," teased Mary Leigh.

Chapter 27

The task force was assembled in FBI Director John Talbot's office. Talbot began the meeting with the question, "All right, folks, let's see where we are at this point. Anyone care to lead off?"

Jane Henson, the psychologist spoke up. "My assessment has not changed since we last met. If anything, my comfort level with the original assessment has increased. The actions of these people are intended to convey a message. From what I see, that message is getting across, although it remains to be seen how long the impact will last. If the situation remains unresolved for a period of time, it will be interesting to see if everyone reverts to their old ways and it is back to business as usual. If that is the case, then I think that you can expect to see some more messages conveyed. There will be more killings."

"Are you saying that you think that the killings are over for the time being?" asked Talbot.

"Yes. I think they are. There hasn't been a killing that we can attribute to our profile in over three weeks and I will be surprised if we have another anytime soon."

"Ed, what's your take on this?"

"I concur completely with Jane's assessment. I have talked with a good number of the members of congress and they are apprehensive and subdued. No one, except for a couple of loud mouths who nobody pays any attention to, are keen on the idea of any new initiatives to involve the government more in everyone's life. I know of some proposed legislation that had been scheduled to be introduced that has been quietly shelved and there are some proposals in committee that have been killed, at least temporarily. I have never seen such a mood in this town."

"Tom, Bill, where are we on the investigations?" asked Talbot.

"Not much further along than we were on day one. The locals have not been able to come up with a single piece of hard evidence or any ideas that would point to someone and, quite frankly, neither have our people. The only thing we have with any hope is that we have matched up the artist's rendition of the possible perp in the Lincoln Johnson murder. There is a guy in Atlanta who is known to possess the skills necessary to pull this sort of thing off. We have his picture on file from his days of government service and when we showed the picture, along with some others, to some people in Harlem, we got a maybe on him. We also got a maybe on one of our people and a definite on the picture of a guy who has been dead for two years. I am flying down to Atlanta tomorrow to see if we can have a conversation with the guy. By the way, his name was not on any of the lists supplied to us by our contacts," said Garrison.

"All right, people, let's stay on it and if anyone comes up with anything that moves the ball, I want to know about it immediately. In the meantime, I'm going to have to advise the Attorney General that we are still treading water and he is not going to be happy but I do think he appreciates what we are up against."

Tom Garrison flew out to Atlanta the next morning on an agency plane and, on arrival, was met by the special agent in charge and one of his agents who advised him that the subject of interest was in town and they had his location. The special agent in charge asked Garrison, "Do you want to try to contact the subject by phone and ask him to come down to the office or possibly meet at a neutral site or just drop in on him?"

"I think it would be best to just drop in on him. I want to see his first reaction when we broach the subject. If you think that he is at home, let's go on over there now."

After about a half hour drive, they were at Joe Rollins's condominium. They knocked on his door and when he opened it, Garrison said, "Mr. Rollins, I am Tom Garrison with the FBI and these two gentlemen are agents from our Atlanta office. Here are our credentials. We would like to talk with you for a few minutes."

Without inviting them in, Rollins said, "And to what do I owe the pleasure of this visit?"

"May we come in?"

"Sure, why not. Make yourself at home."

"Mr. Rollins, we would like to know what you were doing in Harlem about a month ago."

Without changing expression Rollins said, "If I were in Harlem about a month ago, what would be your interest in that information? Have I committed a crime?"

"Mr. Rollins, please just answer the question," said Garrison.

"No. I don't think so, until you tell me what this is about. If you are not prepared to do that, then this conversation is over," said Rollins in a determined manner with a demeanor to match.

"Now look here, Rollins, we are conducting an investigation and if you don't want to be faced with the possibility of an obstruction of justice charge, you will answer this and any other questions we ask," said the young agent who was tagging along.

Tom Garrison was shaking his head as Rollins replied to the brash young agent, "Sonny, you're not dealing with some simpleton off the street who got caught boosting a car and I am totally unimpressed so far, so why don't you leave this to the grownups?"

The special agent in charge placed a hand on the arm of the young agent and with a look told him to keep his mouth shut.

"Mr. Rollins, we are looking into the murder of the Reverend Lincoln Johnson and it has been suggested that you were in town during the period that he was killed. We are merely trying to confirm whether in fact you were or not," said Garrison in a conciliatory tone.

"So, in your round about way, you are trying to determine if I killed him. No, I did not kill him. As to whether I was in town when he was killed I cannot say since I don't even know when he was killed and with that we will conclude this inquiry. If you have any further questions later on, let me know and my attorney will respond."

Joe rose from his chair, signaling the end of the visit and the trio of agents left his condominium. As they were walking back to the car, Garrison said," We're going to check out Mr. Rollins further both here in Atlanta and in New York. On this end I want you to determine whether Mr. Rollins was in town or not when the crime occurred. And get his phone records and credit card receipts for the period including at least thirty days prior and two weeks after the date of Mr. Johnson's demise. I'll take care of the New York end. Mr. Rollins was very difficult to read but he's all we've got at this point."

Garrison flew back to Washington and contacted the New York office. He turned them loose on trying to determine if Rollins had in fact been in New York during the kill period.

G. Lee Greer

Chapter 28

When Peck, Mary Leigh, and Vincent arrived back at the farm from the television studio, they sat in the den, with lunch trays and watched a replay of the tape of the mornings' program which Mr. Briggs had made. They watched it in its entirety, without conversation and when it was concluded, Peck said, "Folks, you have just seen my first and last appearance on a talk show. I am glad I did it and I guess I didn't do too badly, but it is not something I want to do again. I will leave it up to the professional talking heads."

"Peck, don't say that. You were marvelous! We need more of that kind of straight talk and we are sure not going to get it from the politicians. I predict that your appearance is going to be well received and that you are going to be in great demand," said Mary Leigh.

"They can demand all they want but I am not doing that anymore. I didn't feel uncomfortable doing it but I do feel uncomfortable now that it's over. I am just not cut out for that kind of exposure. I want life to be simpler, not more complicated. End of story."

Peck received a number of phone calls from friends and from his proud mother, congratulating him on his appearance and he was embarrassed by all the compliments and attention. Somewhat embarrassed, he accepted their praise graciously but it further fortified his decision to never do that sort of thing again.

"Mary Leigh, is there anything in particular you would like to do this afternoon, or what is left of it? I'm afraid that our weekend is swiftly coming to a close and it has been much too short," said Peck.

"I would love to go down to see the pond and that wonderful cottage again."

Peck blushed. He hoped Vincent wasn't looking at him. The way Mary Leigh had said it conveyed a clear message to Peck that she had more in mind than just looking at the pond and although he liked the idea, he was very uncomfortable in front of Vincent. Vincent had noticed but he tried his best to keep a neutral face, though inside he was beaming.

"Yeah, we can do that," said Peck.

Peck and Mary Leigh spent the rest of the afternoon at the cottage while Vincent lounged around the pool. When the two of them returned to the house and poolside, Vincent found it hard to look at them without grinning, so he excused himself and retired to his room for a rest.

"Peck, when are your returning to New York, tonight or tomorrow?" asked Mary Leigh.

"In the morning. I need to be back by noon but I want you to stay as long as you wish. Mr. and Mrs. Briggs would love your company."

JUSTICE REGAINED

"No, as much as I have enjoyed the weekend and love this place, I will leave when you do. It wouldn't be the same without you here. I hope that you will invite me back again."

"You can count on that and I will make it a point to give you a little more notice next time and if you ever feel the urge to come down here, even if I am not here, just give Mrs. Briggs a call and tell her you are coming. She will love it"

"In the meantime I do not intend to limit our contact to visits to the farm. Every chance I get I will get down to Washington and I hope that you will find your way up to New York on occasion," added Peck, with a hopeful smile on his face.

"My thoughts exactly. The first thing I am going to do when I get back is sit down and reconstruct my calendar, eliminating everything that is not absolutely necessary at the moment. I am going to get into the habit of saying no to a lot of people who place demands on my time. As a result of this weekend, my focus has changed and the focus is now on you and me and the rest of my life and how I want to live it. My life is going to be different from this point forward. I hope that the future includes you but even if it doesn't you have helped me to see what is really important," said Mary Leigh.

"The feeling and thoughts are mutual. Without realizing it at the time, when I placed that call to you, inviting you down for the weekend, my life was unalterably changed for the better. Being with you has helped me to make up my mind to do what I have been fighting for some time and that is to get off the treadmill and enjoy my friends and loved ones for as long as I can," said Peck.

Mary Leigh looked at Peck with eyes of love and admiration and then she said, "You know, Peck, if it wouldn't look so obvious, I would ask you to show me the cottage again." They laughed together.

Chapter 29

The Senate majority leader, Senator Frank Thornton, had called the meeting. Present with him were Senator William Hartley, the designated chairman of the Senate judiciary committee, Senator Ed Jennings, the ranking member of the current judiciary committee and two other senators in the leadership chain.

"I have called this meeting so that we can discuss with Senator Hartley what the party expects of him in his new role as chairman of judiciary before he meets with the full committee tomorrow," said Senator Thorton.

That brought a questioning look to the face of Senator Hartley and the reply, "Are you going to tell me how to do my job?"

"No, but we are going to suggest to you what we feel are ideas that are in the best interests of the party and that we expect you to support the party position. Senator Spenser, while he was too outspoken and, in some cases, too unyielding, was doing what the majority of the party wanted him to do by keeping these conservative and moderate judges bottled up so that we did not have to have an up and down vote on most of them. As you know, most politicians dislike casting votes. If they could they would go through their entire political career without casting a single vote. Every time a vote is cast there are those that are pleased and those that are not pleased. Over time, when you total up all those that are displeased with your votes, it can amount to political trouble and even defeat. The easy way is to just not have to vote on controversial issues and that is where the committee chairmen render such a valuable service to the fellow party members: they just don't allow a vote to come up and the member is not on record, one way or the other, and they can demagogue the issue without taking direct blame. We want you to continue doing what Senator Spenser was doing but in a seemingly more pleasant way. You have been around long enough and know all the rules and tricks to get it done. That is all we are asking," said the majority leader.

They all turned and looked at Senator Hartley and he in turn looked at each of them, directly into their eyes, for what seemed like minutes and then he spoke.

"Senator Thornton, gentlemen, you have the wrong guy for the job and here's what you need to do to remedy the situation. You need to reconvene the caucus tomorrow and explain to them that I am just not going to work out and that they need to elect someone else as chairman of judiciary. You need to go into detail as to why I am not going to work out along the lines of what you have said here today and I will explain to the caucus why I can not do that. If you like, I will cancel the scheduled meeting of full judiciary for tomorrow and allow you time to have your caucus. Is that what you want me to do?" replied Senator Hartley, with a steely edge to his voice and resolve showing on his face.

Senator Thornton was taken aback with the response from Senator Hartley. It was clearly not what he had expected and noticeably perturbed, he said, "Senator Hartley, that is not what we desire and you know it. All we want is for you to be reasonable and cooperative. There is a lot at stake here and you have a responsibility to your party."

"My first and overriding responsibility is to the country, next to the people who sent me here, then to the Senate, and lastly to the party. To the extent that these actions coincide with the interest of my political party so be it, but I will not, I repeat, I will not put the interests of a political party above the interests of the nation. Now, I am going to leave you gentlemen. You have until nine thirty tomorrow morning to notify me as to whether you want me to cancel the meeting of full judiciary. If you decide to caucus, I expect to be notified so that I can be there to present my side of the case. Good day, gentlemen," he said and left the room.

Nine thirty the next morning came and went with no word from Senator Thornton. At ten AM Senator Hartley gaveled the meeting of the full judiciary committee to order and opened the meeting with, "Ladies and gentlemen, we are here today to set the ground rules as to how this committee will operate after the passing of Senator Spenser and my election to replace him as chairman. I have no intention of dictating how we will operate. I am going to leave that up to you. I am going to tell you how I think we should operate and try to make the best case that I can as to why I think we should do so but at the end of the day we will call for a vote and we will determine democratically, by majority vote, whether to adopt those rules or not. If the majority of the committee does not agree with me, then I expect you to offer an alternative and we will vote on that. If that fails, then we will just keep at it until we have adopted rules that the majority of the committee can agree to but be warned, this committee will not conduct the first piece of business until we have agreed to our new rules. Now I would like to hear from each of you who want to speak to the subject before us and I will begin by recognizing the ranking minority member, Senator Paul Welles."

"Mr. Chairman, first let me congratulate you on your election as chairman. I must say that it is like a breath of fresh air and I am optimistic, for the first time in years, that this committee can meet its responsibility in a timely, fair and judicious way. I will reserve further comment at this time and I look forward, with great anticipation to considering your newly proposed rules. Thank you, Mr. Chairman."

"The chair recognizes the ranking majority member, Senator Barbara Goodman."

"Mr. Chairman, let me too offer my congratulations to you on your election as chairman. I am confident that you are prepared to meet your responsibility forthrightly and fairly. I am not sure what you have in mind that would steer us radically away from the time honored rules and tradition that have governed us in the past and I am not convinced that we really need drastic change, however, I will listen attentively along with everyone else and be prepared to speak to any points of concern I have later on. Thank you, Mr. Chairman."

The chairman recognized each of the other members of the committee in alternating order and each of them felt compelled to speak whether they had anything to say or not. The meeting was being televised live by C-Span and the opportunity for posturing was just too great to pass up. The senate judiciary committee is a large committee and it took all the first day just to get in the opening statements of the members. At six o'clock in the evening, Chairman Hartley gaveled the meeting to a recess to be resumed the following morning at ten AM.

The next day, sharply at ten AM, Chairman Hartley gaveled the meeting to order and read a brief statement.

"At this time I am going to present to the committee, for its consideration, a proposed set of rules under which we will operate in the future. I invite your comments and criticisms and if anyone wishes to modify, amend, delete, or add to the language I request that you submit your proposal to me in writing and after we have exhausted all discourse, the chair will present your proposed amendments to the committee for an up or down vote. If anyone wishes to submit a whole set of rules for consideration in lieu of the chair's recommendations, they may do so and that proposal will be considered first. If that motion fails or succeeds we will still present and consider all individual proposals and have an up or down vote. Staff will now distribute to the members the rules which I propose and I invite you to follow along as I read them."

After a brief pause to allow the staff to distribute the written proposal, the Chairman began: "Number one: All nominations received from the President will be scheduled for a hearing within ninety days from date of receipt. Number two: The hearings for nominees to the positions of federal district judges, appellate level judges and lesser appointments will last no more that three days. Number three: The hearings for nominees to the United States Supreme Court will last no more than five days. Number four: A committee vote to recommend or not to recommend will be held and recorded within one week from the close of a hearing. Number five: The recommendation of the committee, with its recorded vote, regardless of whether the committee recommends for or against the nominee, will be forwarded to the senate floor with the request that the full senate vote on the nominee at its earliest convenience."

The chair will now recognize any member who wishes to speak concerning the proposed rules. There was a chorus of "Mr. Chairman," and Chairman Hartley said, "the Chair recognizes the ranking majority member, Senator Goodman."

"Mr. Chairman. I must say that your proposed rules are a radical departure from the time honored rules and traditions of the committee and it is exactly what I feared most. Our role is severely diminished and it seems to me to be completely unnecessary."

"Senator Goodman, the time honored rules and traditions of the committee that you speak of is nothing more than the rules adopted at the time by the committee sitting in the majority. There has been no evolution of rules but merely the adoption of rules to suit the sitting members at the time. The proposed rules are not adopted in perpetuity and are not binding on future committees. The makeup of committees and the chairmanship changes from time to time and after each change the committee is free to adopt new rules as it sees fit. All I am suggesting here is a set of rules under which the current committee will operate. Do you have an objection to any specific rule that I have proposed?"

"Not at this time, Mr. Chairman."

"The chair recognizes the ranking minority member, Senator Welles.

"Mr. Chairman, what you are proposing is exactly what I have been advocating for years. Every nominee deserves a timely and fair hearing and after we have done our investigation of the nominee and held a hearing, allowing all persuasions to render their concerns and opinions, we have a solemn responsibility to make a recommendation to our colleagues in the full senate. It is then their collective responsibility to accept or reject the recommendation of the committee. I would not change a single word of your proposal and I am prepared for an up or down vote on the new rules whenever the chair calls for it. I will not waste any more of the committee's time. Thank you, Mr. Chairman."

Again every member of the committee felt compelled to speak eloquently on the merits of the proposal. The viewpoints divided along predictable lines, with the radical, left wing extremists registering deep concerns about the proposed rules but they tempered their remarks because it became obvious early on that the moderate members of their own party were going to support the proposal and they were going to take a drubbing. Their rhetoric was merely for the benefit of the narrow special interests whom they depended on.

It was nearing five o'clock when the members of the committee had exhausted themselves and the chairman declared that they would recess for the day and reconvene the next day for the purpose of voting on the proposed rules and any amendments thereto.

When the question on the adoption of the proposed rules was called for the next morning, the ayes prevailed overwhelmingly with only three dissenting votes. There were two amendments offered, both intended to water down the effect of the rules. They failed by the same vote.

"Ladies and gentlemen of the committee, we have now set the rules by which we will conduct our business and we have a lot of work to do in the coming days and weeks. We have a substantial backlog of nominees to get to and there will be more coming, so we are going to dig right in and see if we can make a dent in the job ahead of us. I will post a schedule for hearing dates on the nominees we have before us now and notify the President of that schedule. We are adjourned, said Chairman Hartley.

Chapter 30

Peck phoned his mother and after chatting for a few minutes he asked her, "Mother, do you remember Mrs. Clara Edwards? Her maiden name was Gregorie."

"Why sure I do. She and I were best friends growing up. She moved to Charleston when she married and I continued to see her when she would return to Beaufort to visit her folks but since her parents passed away years ago, we sort of lost touch with each other. She still has a lot of family here in Beaufort."

"Do you remember a daughter named Mary Leigh?" asked Peck.

"Yes. She used to spend a good part of the summer here in Beaufort with her grandparents. I believe you and she are about the same age. I remember that she married well and moved away, I think, to Washington. Why do you ask?"

"Mother, I have begun to see Mary Leigh socially. She has been a widow now for about five years and I finally gathered up my courage and asked to see her."

"Peck, that is wonderful. I haven't seen Mary Leigh since she was a teenager but I remember that she was a pretty young girl with a sweet disposition and I know that she comes from good family."

"The reason I mentioned all this is that I thought about maybe bringing Mary Leigh down for a visit. I know that she would love it and I would like for you, Sarah, and Bill to meet her again. Do you think that that would be all right?"

"Peck, that would be marvelous! We have plenty of room and I know that everyone would love to see her. When are you thinking of coming down?"

"I really don't know, mother. I haven't said anything to Mary Leigh about this and I will have to ask her and find out when she can get away but I promise to do that immediately and let you know as soon as possible. In the meantime, I know that as soon as we hang up you are going to get on the phone and tell Sarah and Bill all about Mary Leigh and that's all right but I would not want it spread all over town, so if you could, let's just keep it in the family for the time being. Okay?"

"Okay, son. You have my word but you are asking an awful lot of this old lady to sit on this wonderful news."

"I know, mother, and I appreciate it. Now I need to go. I will be back in touch soon and I love you."

"I love you too, son. Goodbye."

When Mrs. Reynolds hung up the phone, she just sat there quietly with tears of joy streaming down her cheeks. She was so happy. She would not worry quite as much about her boy Peck anymore.

Peck lifted the receiver again and called Mary Leigh. Mary Leigh answered on the second ring and said, "Hello Peck."

"How did you know it was me?" asked Peck.

"When I returned from the farm I put your office, home and farm numbers into my speed dial system and with caller I.D. I knew that it was you calling from your office."

"Remind me to give you my car phone number too and then I will never be out of reach," said Peck, with a chuckle.

"I am so glad that you called. I was worried that you might be one of those fellows who uses a girl and then forgets her forever."

"There is not much chance of that. I have been unable to think about anything else and my business is suffering. I can't get anything done. You just may be personally responsible for a two point dip in the market today."

"Ah, such power. I will have to be careful how I use it," answered Mary Leigh.

"I spoke with my mother today and I told her about you. She remembered you from the days when you used to spend time with your grandparents. I suggested to her that I would like to bring you down for a visit and she was thrilled. If you don't go, you are going to break an old lady's heart."

"Oh, Peck, I would love to go. You just tell me when and I'll get packed. You know, I still have a lot of relatives in Beaufort that I haven't seen in a long time. I hope that we can stay long enough for me to visit around."

"We will stay as long as you like. I thought you may want to drive up to Charleston and visit with your mother while you are down there."

"Peck, just let me know when and the sooner the better."

"What about this Friday afternoon. Is that soon enough? We can plan on staying for a week plus, through Sunday of the following week."

"Let me get busy canceling everything during that period. I will be ready when you are. How are we going to get down there and where will I meet up with you?"

"We will be flying down on my plane. Why don't you drive down to the farm Friday afternoon and Vincent and I will fly in to the landing strip nearby and pick you up. Mr. Briggs can drive you over to the strip."

"I have a better idea, said Mary Leigh. Why don't we meet at the farm on Thursday and spend Thursday night at the farm and you can show me that cute little cottage down by the pond? Then we can go on to Beaufort Friday afternoon."

Smiling, Peck said, "I like the way you think, Mary Leigh. Let me see if I can work that out. I will be back to you shortly."

Peck rang Vincent and asked him to come in to his office. Vincent was there almost immediately.

"Vincent, you look like you need a vacation. What do you think about us going down home Friday afternoon and staying until Sunday of the following week? We haven't taken that much time off in years."

"That sounds great to me. It will be good to spend some time with my folks. I know they will be pleased," replied Vincent.

"All right. Here's the plan. We have the closing on the Powers project on Friday morning. You can handle that without me, right? I will have Gil fly me down to the farm on Thursday afternoon. He will return to pick you up on Friday afternoon and then return to the strip at the farm. From there we will go on down to Beaufort. Does that sound like a plan?"

"Sounds great, boss. I'm looking forward to it."

"Oh, by the way, Vincent, Mary Leigh will be going down with us," Peck said, sheepishly.

"Uh, sir, I don't want to be in the way. Maybe I should just hang around here and look after things and you and Mrs. Braxton just go on down and enjoy yourselves," said Vincent.

"Look, Vincent, let's get something straight once and for all. It would seem that Mary Leigh is going to be a regular part of my life from now on but that in no way affects our relationship. If I ever need some private time, I will tell you but unless I do, you will continue to assume that I asked you along because I wanted to and it does not make me uncomfortable. Are we together on this?"

"Yes, sir. I understand and I'm glad Mrs. Braxton is going with us."

"Don't let her hear you call her Mrs. Braxton. You have already been warned," said Peck, with a grin.

Peck called his mother and advised her of the plans and then called Mary Leigh again.

When she answered, he said, "Your extra day added to our trip will work out nicely so I will see you at the farm on Thursday and I must say that I am looking forward to it with feverish anticipation."

Mary Leigh didn't reply for a few seconds and then she said, "Peck, would you like to try for Wednesday?"

Peck laughed and said, "Goodbye, Mary Leigh."

G. Lee Greer

Chapter 31

The task force was assembled in Director Talbot's conference room. Talbot said, "Tom, why don't you lead off and tell us what you have."

"Mr. Director, I wish I had something positive to tell you, but, quite frankly, we are stymied. We have not been able to latch on to anything that would give us cause to proceed more vigorously against anyone. We believe that the guy from Atlanta, Joe Rollins, was in New York during the time of Johnson's death but we can't prove it conclusively. We checked every hotel and rooming house in the area and cannot come up with a clerk who remembers him. We checked the registrations of all the ins and outs one week prior to and one week after the date of the killing and his name did not pop up. Of course, he could have registered under an assumed name. We cannot prove or disprove that he was at home in Atlanta during the time of the killing. We checked his credit cards and there was a gasoline purchase in Atlanta two days after the killing. His previous usage of the card was six days prior to the last purchase, in Atlanta, which is pretty normal. His phone records revealed nothing. In my personal visit to Mr. Rollin's home I found him to be calm and calculating but I did not get a feel, one way or the other, about him. I can tell you that he is a very smart man and he is not going to say or do anything to help us make a case against him."

Garrison continued, "The Driscoll case in Boston has been a dead end from the start. You know that he was gay and the word is that he had a lot of liaisons with a lot of different people. Even though he was a public figure, highly recognized, he had a habit of striking out on his own to places and with people unknown. Our people in Boston are theorizing that somehow the killer lured him to the beach that night for what he thought would be a sexual encounter and then popped him. It is all conjecture, of course."

"All of the other cases are dry wells also. We just haven't been able to come up with anything to hang our hat on. The locals are just as frustrated as we are and everyone is still digging but I am not too hopeful. The perpetrator or perpetrators are real pros and they planned and executed well and left no trail," Garrison finished his report.

"I can attest to that, said Bill Sisson, the forensics specialist. We have eight murders, eight crime scenes and not the first piece of evidence to look at. It is incredible. I have never encountered crime scenes so clean.

"Have you checked out all the pros that our contacts provided to us. Are we able to account for all of them and their time and movements during the killings?" asked Talbot.

JUSTICE REGAINED

"Yes sir, we have. They were all dead ends also," said Garrison.

"Ed, what is the mood around town and what is being said?" asked Talbot.

"Mr. Director, the mood is sober and reflective. It's almost like no one wants to talk about it. Except for a couple of predictable blowhards, no one is seeking out the media, as they normally would, to make pronouncements and lament the state of affairs in this nation. I would say that if the purpose of the killings was to intimidate and cow the politicians and the spokespersons for the activists, then they have succeeded, at least temporarily. It is certainly not business as usual in this town. There is even talk of ending the congressional session by early November so that everyone can go home and let this thing die down. There is also some grumbling, though not publicly, about the ineptness and inefficiency of law enforcement and their inability to make a case against anyone. On the other side I listened in on a conversation between a couple of congressman, a cabinet official and a senator and the consensus was that this whole thing was being orchestrated by some very smart people, using the very best talent and they were not optimistic that this thing would ever get resolved and that they were going to have to operate in this atmosphere for a good while to come. Again, if Jane's profile assessment is correct, and I believe that it is, the people behind this have achieved their purpose."

"Does anyone else have anything to add?" asked Talbot. They all looked from one to another but no one spoke.

"Then the question becomes: Where do we go from here?" Again there was silence.

"Folks, we can not just close up shop and go our merry way. At least, for the time being, we have to appear to be doing something. I need some ideas or at least one idea that will give us some direction," pleaded Talbot.

Ed Gorman spoke up. "I'm probably the least qualified one in the room to suggest anything about investigative procedure but it seems to that we should take these killings one at a time, choose one, if you will, and marshall all our resources, time and effort and apply them to that one case. If we come up dry on that one then we choose another, etc., etc., etc. In the meantime I think that we can assume that the local jurisdictions will continue to work the cases and they may get lucky and come up with something."

Talbot looked around the room, inviting comment. Tom Garrison spoke up saying, "Ed has a point, considering our success, or lack thereof, so far. The question becomes; which case shall we concentrate on first?"

Jane Henson spoke up. "Why don't we begin at the beginning and look at the Judge Hammond case? We have jurisdiction so we don't have to take the case away from the locals."

Again Talbot looked around the room and hearing no comment said," All right. The Hammond case it is. Tom, Bill, it looks like the two of you are going to set up shop in Buffalo and you should have extra incentive to solve the case before the hard winter and six foot snowdrifts set in. Tom, you will take the lead, of course, and you let me know if you need anything. Thank you, people. That will do it for the day."

Chapter 32

On Thursday afternoon Vincent drove Peck out to the strip for the flight down to the farm. When they arrived at the airstrip, Peck said, "Vincent, why don't you try to get away by three tomorrow. That should get you down by four o'clock. I will have Mr. Briggs drive Mary Leigh and me out to the strip and meet you there. We will be packed up and ready to go when you arrive and we'll head on down to Beaufort."

"Sounds good, boss. I will see you around four tomorrow."

When Peck arrived at the strip near the farm, Mr. Briggs was waiting for him and they made their way out to the farm. Mary Leigh had already arrived and was visiting with Mrs. Briggs when Peck walked in.

"I hope that you are not spending this time alone with Mrs. Briggs trying to lure her away from me," Peck said as he greeted Mary Leigh with a kiss on the cheek.

"Hello, Peck. I have given it my best shot, but I am ready to throw in the towel. For some strange reason she has this sense of loyalty to you that I have not been able to shake loose."

"What time would you like dinner tonight?" a smiling Mrs. Briggs inquired.

"Why don't we plan on eight o'clock? Mary Leigh and I are going to tramp around the property for awhile but we will be ready for your delicious dinner by eight," said Peck.

"Mary Leigh, I'm going to change clothes real quickly and if you want to change, why don't we meet out back in about fifteen minutes? Will that give you enough time?"

"I'll be waiting," said Mary Leigh, as she headed out to her room.

Peck and Mary Leigh piled into the pickup truck and headed out. They drove around the property for a short while and then headed for the pond and the cottage.

"This was a great idea, Mary Leigh. I am glad that you were not shy about suggesting it. I was wondering how and when we would be able to be together again because I know that we will not be able to cuddle closely while we are in Beaufort."

"I'm glad too, Peck. I have been looking forward to this since you called. I feel so young and alive again. I was reflecting on our new relationship and regretting that we have wasted so much time these last few years but I understand why and it makes our time now so much more special. I hope that we will make the most of it."

"We will, Mary Leigh," said Peck as they arrived at the cottage.

When they entered the cottage, they both noticed a beautiful fresh cut flower arrangement on the coffee table. They looked at each other and smiled and knew that they were not fooling anyone.

"Mrs. Briggs is a very perceptive and understanding lady. I guess that we gave ourselves away right off the bat. Does that bother you?" asked Peck.

"Not in the least. I think that it is sweet and my estimate and respect for her, which was already pretty high, just went up further," said Mary Leigh.

They clasped hands and entered the bedroom.

After a sumptuous dinner they sat in the den and enjoyed after dinner drinks and conversation with Mr. and Mrs. Briggs whom Peck had insisted join them.

Around ten o'clock Mr. Briggs said, "We old folks need our rest, so we will say goodnight. We will see you tomorrow and thank you for inviting us to join you. We enjoyed your company."

After the Briggs's had departed Peck suggested that they take a short stroll around before retiring. As they walked Peck said, "Since our little secret has been exposed and since the Briggs's quarters are in the opposite wing of the house, far away from our rooms, and since I know that it will be awhile until we are able to be alone again, if you hear someone enter your room later on, do not be frightened. It will just be me, who just cannot seem to get enough of you. If your door is locked, I will know that you have tired of me already and I will slink back to my room to dream of what might have been."

"We are both shameless. I was thinking the same thing and if you had not stated your intentions, I would probably have visited you in your room," said Mary Leigh, as she stopped and embraced Peck for a long time, not saying anything but content to be in his arms.

When the plane flew in Friday afternoon, Peck and Mary Leigh were waiting and in minutes they were airborne for Beaufort. On arriving, Peck's sister, Sarah, was there to greet them. Bill was off on another errand.

"Sarah, I would like for you to meet Mary Leigh Braxton. Mary Leigh, my sister, Sarah." They embraced and you could see the genuineness of their greeting and instant like for each other. After Sarah had hugged Peck and Vincent, they loaded up and headed to the house. On arrival, Mother Reynolds, Bill, and Vincent's parents were waiting on the front porch to greet them.

"Mom, this is Mary Leigh," said Peck.

Mrs. Reynolds opened her arms and embraced Mary Leigh and said, "I am so glad to see you again after all these years. You are even more beautiful than I remembered you as a teenage girl and I am so happy that you and Peck are seeing each other. Welcome to our home and if you all will come inside, I have a surprise for you."

When they entered the house, Mary Leigh's mouth flew open and she was speechless. There stood her mother, Clara Edwards.

When she finally gained her composure, Mary Leigh said, "Mother what are you doing here?" as she raced to embrace her.

"Elizabeth called me and after reminiscing for ages she invited me down to visit while you are here. She even had Bill drive up to bring me down, so here I am. It is so good that you are here. It's been nearly six months since I have seen you," said Mrs. Edwards.

"Mother, I would like for you to meet or meet again after all these years Peck Reynolds," said Mary Leigh.

Peck stepped forward and Mrs. Edwards embraced him and said, "I was so pleased when Mary Leigh told me that she and you were seeing each other. You have made two old ladies very happy and to be here in your mother's home and visiting with her is a thrill. I don't know why we all didn't think of this a lot earlier."

They all laughed together and went into the spacious living room and began to chatter.

Mary Leigh pulled Mother Reynolds aside and said, "I can't tell you how much I appreciate your inviting my mother down to visit. It just makes a wonderful trip even more special."

"Well, I was thinking of you and Peck but I had a selfish motive too. Your mother and I were very close as childhood friends and it gave us the opportunity to renew our acquaintance and friendship now that we have something in common. We have both vowed to remain in close touch. You and Peck just gave us a good reason to reacquaint ourselves," said mother Reynolds.

The week was filled with good times. Mary Leigh and her mother spent a lot of time visiting with their relatives, sometimes with Peck and Mrs. Reynolds in tow.

Georgi and Anna Havel were thrilled to have Vincent home. They hadn't spent this much time with him since he had moved north. Vincent felt himself relaxing and a feeling of peace and contentment came over him that he had not known since his wife and child had died. He was feeling what Peck was feeling, that family and home were the most important things in one's life and he silently vowed to himself that he was going to devote himself to maintaining that feeling, whatever it took.

As they sat quietly in the Havel's quarters Anna said "Tell us about Mrs. Braxton. Mrs. Reynolds gave us the background of the early years but we want to know how they came to be together after all these years."

"They have known each other for a long time. She and Mrs. Reynolds were good friends and they used to see a lot of each other until Mrs. Reynolds died. A short time later, Mrs. Braxton's husband died and they lost touch with each other, except on occasion. Mr. Reynolds ran into her again a few weeks ago and they have been seeing each other since, as time allows. I believe that they are head over heels in love with each other and it would not surprise me if they got married in the near future but please don't mention this to Mr. Reynolds. I can tell you that he is a changed man since he started seeing her. He is the same man now that we knew all those years before Mrs. Reynolds became ill and died. It makes me feel good to see him so happy again," said Vincent.

"And what about you, Vincent? Are you ready to get on with your life? Your father and I have worried about you, as I am sure you know. Maybe you can learn one more thing from the major. You see what a difference it has made in him," said Anna Havel, with a mother's concern in her eyes.

"Maybe you are right, Mother. I'm going to have to think about that and who knows what will happen," said Vincent.

"I know that you don't want your poor mother meddling in your life and I promise not to do that after I make this one suggestion, if you are willing to listen."

"You know that I cannot refuse you, Mother, and on the promise that you will not meddle I will hear your suggestion."

"Good. Do you remember Carolyn Spencer from your high school days? She was a couple of years behind you in school but I know that back then she had a big crush on you. Well, she still lives here in Beaufort. Her husband died a few years ago and after that she opened a dress shop downtown. Every time I go in there, she asks about you. She is a beautiful woman, sweet and honest. Everybody in the community likes her, including a number of eligible bachelors who have tried to woo her but she doesn't seem interested in any of them. I think that she is saving herself for my Vincent."

Georgi Havel chuckled and said, "Vincent, mark down the time and date of this moment. This is the point at which you have been compromised by a devious woman and from this point forward there is no hope for you. I will admit, however, that your mother's assessment of the lady in question is right on the money and if I were not happily married to your mother I would have made a run on her myself."

"You both are impossible but I thank you for your suggestion. Let me think about it," replied Vincent.

The next day, while Mary Leigh and her mother were visiting relatives, Anna Havel asked Vincent to drive her downtown so that she could run a couple of errands and they asked Mrs. Reynolds and Peck to go with them. They both agreed and when downtown Vincent and Peck walked around while their mothers were running their errands. When they met back at the car, Anna said that she had just one more stop to make and then they could return home.

"Where to, mother?" asked Vincent.

"I need to stop by the dress shop. It won't take but a minute."

Vincent grinned and shook his head and said, "You are a devious woman, mother, just like father said." Vincent then explained to Peck what his mother had said the night before. Apparently Mrs. Reynolds had already been briefed by Anna.

"Vincent, you have been had. You might as well reconcile yourself to your fate," said Peck.

When they arrived and parked at the dress shop, Anna insisted that Vincent and Peck go in with them. When they politely declined, Anna argued that she would probably have some heavy packages to carry and she would need Vincent's help. As Mrs. Reynolds and Peck Grinned from ear to ear, Vincent acceded and the four of them entered the shop. When Carolyn Spencer saw Mrs. Havel she came immediately and greeted her and Mrs. Reynolds.

"Carolyn, this is my son, Vincent. Do you remember him?"

Carolyn looked at Vincent and smiling, stepped forward and offered her hand to Vincent and said, "Vincent, it is so good to see you after all these years."

Vincent was stunned. She was a beautiful woman and he could not take his eyes off of her. Peck poked him in the ribs and said, "I believe this is the point where you are supposed to say that you are glad to see her too."

Vincent said to Carolyn, "Forgive me. I am pleased to see you too. I remember you now from high school. You were a cheerleader, right?"

"Yes, I was. I didn't know that you noticed. How are you, Vincent?"

"I am well, thank you, and enjoying my visit with the folks and just being home again."

The two of them chatted for a few more minutes as Anna, Mrs. Reynolds, and Peck drifted away from them. Vincent did not notice their absence until he turned to speak to his mother and noticed that they were on the other side of the store smiling at the two of them.

"Mother, are you ready to go? Carolyn, if you will show me the packages I will take them to the car."

Carolyn looked perplexed and Anna said, "Oh, don't worry about the packages. Carolyn will have them brought out. Goodbye, Carolyn. It was so nice to see you." She then headed for the door.

"Goodbye, Carolyn. I'm glad that I got the chance to see you," Vincent said as he offered his hand.

"Goodbye, Vincent. I hope to see you again before you leave town."

When they were all back in the car there was complete silence until Vincent said, "Mother, there never were any packages, were they?"

The other three broke out in laughter and soon Vincent joined in. They were still laughing when they arrived back at the house.

G. Lee Greer

Chapter 33

To everyone's regret, the visit was coming to a close. It was Friday and Peck, Mary Leigh, and Vincent would be leaving on Sunday and Bill would be driving Mrs. Edwards back to Charleston. They were all sitting around after dinner talking about what a grand week it had been and with Mother Reynolds, Mrs. Havel, and Mrs. Edwards trying to persuade them to stay a little longer.

"I'm afraid that Vincent and I need to get back to New York for some appointments on Monday but I promise that we will be back again very soon and Mary Leigh will be with us if at all possible," said Peck.

"Clara and I are going to insist that you do that. On Saturday evening for dinner we are going to have an old fashioned low country Frogmore stew. Georgi has become something of an expert in cooking Frogmore stew and he has agreed to cook for us," said Mother Reynolds.

There was unanimous agreement that that was a perfect ending to the visit, with Mary Leigh saying, "I haven't eaten Frogmore stew in twenty five years."

Mrs. Havel said, "Vincent, maybe you would like to invite Carolyn to join us for dinner."

Vincent looked at everyone and they were all grinning. He said, "I see that the conspiracy continues but it so happens that I had already decided to invite her to dinner, though I haven't done so yet. With your permission, Mother, I will go call her now."

Everyone applauded as Vincent left the room. He returned a few minutes later and with a straight face and disappointed look said, "Carolyn has a previous engagement Saturday evening and will be unable to join us."

Mrs. Havel was clearly distressed with the news and the others displayed looks of disappointment. Vincent let it sink in for a short while longer and then grinning said, "I was just kidding. I am going to pick Carolyn up around seven."

"Vincent Havel, you are still not too old for a spanking, you know," Mrs. Havel said as she rose and hugged Vincent's neck, much to the delight of the others.

On Saturday Georgi Havel spent all day shopping for the ingredients, setting up the cooker and preparing the food for cooking with Vincent and Peck serving as assistants. Frogmore stew is a favorite in the coastal region of South Carolina. It is a mixture of smoked sausage, potatoes, corn on the cob, and shrimp and usually cooked outside on a propane burner. The recipe is simple: Fill a large container about half way full with water, bring it to a boil, and add a mixed spice seasoning. Add potatoes and bring it back to a boil and cook for ten minutes, add the sausage and corn and cook for another ten minutes or until the potatoes are tender, then add the shrimp and cook for another three to five minutes or until the shrimp are pink. It is served up with a favorite bread and drink, usually beer or iced tea.

Shortly after seven Vincent returned with Carolyn. She was greeted warmly by everyone and she was glowing. Vincent was clearly in awe of her and could not wipe the smile off his face. Though she spent some time with the ladies she devoted most of her time and attention to Vincent and he loved every minute of it.

The dinner was a huge success and afterward they all sat around lamenting the fact that they had eaten too much. Vincent and Carolyn left around ten and Mother Reynolds, Mrs. Edwards and the Havels retired for the evening. Peck, Mary Leigh, Sarah and her husband, Bill and his wife, Vincent's younger brother Henri and his wife sat around and talked about what a great time everyone had had and that they needed to enjoy these type occasions more often. It had been a notable ten days in many respects.

On Sunday, they parted company with a good feeling and with the knowledge that the best was yet to come.

G. Lee Greer

Chapter 34

It was late November and congress had adjourned for the year. Everyone had headed home, leaving Washington to the bureaucrats and the executive branch. The special task force assembled by the Attorney General was still hard at work on their mission. They had reconvened in the conference room of FBI Director John Talbot for an update.

"Okay, Tom, lead us off," said Talbot.

"We have worked our way through the first five; Judge Hammond, Goldstone, Wiley, Driscoll, and Dunning. I'm afraid that we are no closer than we were before. We have determined that in the Dunning case there was a stranger in town at the approximate time of the killing, a woman who was just traveling through town. According to the owner of a local café in Pelham, the woman was passing through on her way to Nashville. No one else saw her, as best as we can determine, and there is no description of the vehicle she was driving. We are at a dead end on that one too, but we are continuing to ask around in hope that someone else may have spotted her or a strange vehicle," said Garrison.

"We are on the Johnson killing now and we're continuing to pursue the Rollins angle. Bill has come up with a determination on the weapon used. Bill, why don't you give us what you have on the weapon?"

"In studying the autopsy report and viewing photographs we can say with some degree of certainty that the weapon, a knife, was a specialty knife, not your run of the mill street knife. It was extremely sharp, like a scalpel and longer that usual. With the least bit more of pressure, the killer could have easily decapitated the victim. It is the type of weapon preferred by special ops people for close up work. It just reinforces the notion that it was a professional hit and makes the Rollins character, or someone like him with a similar background, look more likely. In taking a closer look at the lock on Johnson's condo, we can also state, with reasonable certainty, that the lock was picked for entry. There are markings on the core of the lock that could not have been made with a key. Again, it just reinforces the theory that we are dealing with a professional," said Sisson.

"Our local agents in New York are continuing to scour the neighborhood to try to put Rollins, or someone like him at the scene within the timeframe. I am headed back up there as soon as we get out of here and plan to give it at least another week and then go on to the Spenser case," said Garrison.

"All right Tom, Bill, stay with it. We are coming up on the holiday season and I want you all to take a reasonable amount of time off and enjoy the season but stick with it and let's try to complete this phase of the investigation by the end of January, unless something significant pops up," said Talbot.

"Jane, Ed, do either of you have anything to add?" asked Talbot.

They both shook their heads no.

"We probably won't be back together before Christmas so I will take the opportunity now to thank all of you and wish you a merry Christmas and a happy new year. Of course, it would be the happiest of new years if we could make a breakthrough on this thing but all we can do is to keep plugging away and hope. Thank you again and I will see you sometime after the first of the year," said Talbot as he rose to end the meeting.

G. Lee Greer

Chapter 35

Peck was enjoying having Mary Leigh visiting him in New York. They were enjoying the holiday season and Mary Leigh was doing some serious shopping. Peck had done some serious shopping also for a very significant gift for Mary Leigh and other gifts for the family in Beaufort. They had just returned to the apartment from dinner and were relaxing and recapping their day.

"Peck, I have significantly contributed to the well being of the New York economy and am now finished with all my Christmas shopping. How about you? Were you able to find everything you wanted?" asked Mary Leigh.

"Yes. I'm finished too. I haven't done this much shopping in ten years and I enjoyed it. For the first time since Phyllis passed away I am looking forward to Christmas. I will give you the credit for that. There are only ten days left until Christmas. What do you think about spending Christmas in Beaufort?" asked Peck.

"I was hoping you were going to suggest that. I love your family and it will give me the chance to spend a couple of days in

Charleston with mother too. I would like for you to go with me, if you will. When do you plan on going down?"

"Why don't we plan on going down on Friday? That will give us a week until Christmas and we can plan on staying until after New Years, if you like. That will give us over two weeks with the folks."

"Peck, that is wonderful. I will call mother tonight. I know that she will be thrilled. If we are leaving on Friday I am going to need to scoot back down home tomorrow and get a couple of things done and get packed up and ready to go."

"Although, I will miss you awfully, that will work out fine. I have a couple of things I need to get done too. Vincent and I will fly into the strip near the farm on Friday afternoon around four. You can drive down to the farm, leave your car at the house, and have Mr. Briggs drive you out to the strip to meet us and before you suggest it, I cannot come down a day early on Thursday. I have to be here Thursday evening for a very important meeting."

Mary Leigh smiled and said, "You don't love me anymore."

"You know, come to think of it, I don't believe that I have ever told you that I love you in those exact words and I do. I love you very much. These few short months since we found each other have meant everything to me. I have something I want to give you. I had planned on giving it to you on Christmas day but I want you to have it now." said Peck.

"I love gifts. Where is it?" Mary Leigh said gleefully.

"You just sit right where you are and I will be back in seconds," said Peck as he rose and went into the bedroom. He was back in seconds and handed the gift to Mary Leigh.

It was a small package, tastefully wrapped, and he gave it to her as he sat down beside her.

Mary Leigh carefully removed the bow and tore into the wrapping. It was a small jeweler's case and she opened it to find a three carat solitary diamond.

"Oh, Peck."

"Mary Leigh, I want to marry you. I want us to spend every day for the rest of our lives together as one and I do not want to wait. I realize that we have only been seeing each other for a few months but I have never been more sure of anything in my life and it just doesn't make sense to draw this thing out for a long time, as long as you feel as I do."

With tears streaming down her face Mary Leigh replied, "Peck, I love you too, very deeply, and since that first day down at the farm, I have being dreaming and hoping for this very moment. You have made me the happiest person alive and yes, I will marry you and the sooner the better. They embraced and kissed for a long time and then Mary Leigh said, "Peck, I have just one request. I want us to be married at the farm."

"I was thinking the same thing." said Peck.

"Mary Leigh, before we go any further I need to tell you of some plans I have and see if you agree."

Mary Leigh nodded anxiously and Peck continued. "I have very quietly entered into negotiations with some people to sell Reynolds Commerce. I haven't even told my family yet and they have just as much interest in the business as I do. I plan to discuss it with them while we are down there Christmas. I would also like for us to move back home to Beaufort. We can buy or build any kind of house you want but I just want to go home. I am out of place here and I am homesick."

"Peck, darling, it is getting even more perfect. I want to go home too and as soon as I get home tomorrow, I will call an agent and put my place on the market."

"Peck, may I call mother and tell her?" continued Mary Leigh excitedly.

"If you do that, then I am going to have to call mother and tell her. Why don't we wait and surprise them when we go down on Friday. Maybe we can get your mother to come down on Friday too and we will tell them all at the same time. If you like, I will call mother and tell her we will be coming down and ask her to call your mother and insist that she come down also. You can call your mother and encourage her to accept the invitation. How does that sound?"

"That is a wonderful plan. Oh, Peck, I am so excited. What a Christmas we are going to have."

"If you don't mind, I would like to call Vincent and ask him to come over now so that we can tell him. He is like a son to me and I have been closer to him than anyone else these last few years. He's only a block away. What do you think?" said Peck.

"Call him. We have to tell someone and Vincent is perfect."

Peck called Vincent and in a short while he was at Peck's apartment. When he entered the living room Mary Leigh jumped up and hugged him fiercely and then held out her hand to show him the ring.

"I have asked Mary Leigh to marry me and she has accepted. You are the only one who knows. We are going to tell everyone else at Christmas," said Peck.

Smiling broadly, Vincent said, "This is perfect. I could not be happier for the both of you. I just knew that it was going to be but I had no idea that it would be this soon. Congratulations!"

"We'll be working on our wedding plans the next couple of weeks but I want you to know now that I want you to be my best man."

"I would be honored, boss," Vincent said as he embraced Peck and he realized that he had never done that before and it felt right.

Peck was visibly moved also and he stammered, "Let me tell you the plan for the holidays because you are included. He went on to tell Vincent of the travel plans and admonished him not to say anything to his parents about the engagement."

After a toast with champagne, Vincent left and Peck said, "Mary Leigh, I am going to call mother and tell her we will be coming. Why don't you call your mother too and then we'll go into the bedroom and pretend that we are at the cottage."

G. Lee Greer

Chapter 36

Tom Garrison was in New York working with the local office, trying to find some kind of link between the Johnson killing and Joe Rollins. It was old fashioned detective work, pounding the streets, going door to door, and talking with people who may have seen a stranger in town during the time of the killing. They showed Joe Rollins's picture around along with some others in the hope that someone would give them a positive identification on Rollins or point them towards someone else. At the real estate office where Joe had inquired, the lady realtor was pretty sure that the picture of Rollins was the same guy who had visited her office and made inquiry about rentals and sales units.

"It kind of looks like the guy, but I cannot be sure. I do remember that he was a big man," said the realtor.

"Did he say anything? Did he ask any questions about anyone?" asked Garrison.

"I believe that he said that he was thinking about moving back to New York but other than that, I don't recall anything else," said the realtor.

"Well, thank you for your time. Here is my card. If you think of anything else, please give me a call," said the agent with Garrison as they exited.

Later in the day they ended up at the Gentlemen's Club and were talking to the bartender. The local agents had visited here earlier but had not turned up anything. They knew that Rev. Johnson had been in the club the night of his death and that there had been some trouble with his girlfriends. They showed Rollin's picture to the bartender who seemingly studied it carefully.

"I don't recognize this guy and I think I would remember him. He is a mean looking dude," said the bartender. In fact, he had recognized him immediately but he wasn't about to give up a brother to the feds or any other cops.

"Would you mind letting the other employees look at the photo?" asked the agent.

"No, not at all," the bartender said as he called over a couple of waitresses and the doorman/bouncer.

"These gentlemen want to show you a photo and see if any of you recognize the guy", the bartender said as he looked at the employees in such a way as to let them know that they were not to be too cooperative.

The agent passed the photo around to all of the employees and they all replied no. Garrison picked up on the look that the bartender had given them but he said nothing. They thanked everyone and left.

"It looks like another dead end day," said the agent with Garrison, as they stood outside the club.

"Maybe not. I am convinced that the bartender recognized the photo and maybe one or more of the others did also but they are not willing to give him up. I believe that Rollins was in the club at some time but that still does not place him at the crime scene or for that matter, in New York at the time of the killing. I believe that there's a very distinct possibility that our Mr. Rollins killed Rev. Johnson but we are a long way away from proving anything," said Garrison.

"Do you want to go back in and see if we can apply a little heat to those people?" asked the agent.

"No. That would not do any good. I am going to head back to Washington for a few days, but I want you to talk with all those people, except the bartender, off premises. See if maybe their memory is any better without the bartender staring them down. I also want you to follow up with the security people at Rev. Johnson's building. Our killer had to gain entry somehow, unless he lives there, and we need to know how he did it. Give them a good look at Rollin's photo too. Maybe we will get lucky. We are damn sure due a break on this thing," said Garrison.

After dropping Garrison off at the airport, the agent returned to Rev. Johnson's building where he met the local detective who was working the case. They met with the chief of security for the building, a retired city policeman.

"We are trying to determine how the perpetrator gained entry to the building. Tell us again all the ways one could gain entry to the building," said the FBI agent.

"There are only three ways in and out of this building; the front entrance, the garage, and the utility entrance. Through the front entrance, only residents or approved guests are admitted. Deliveries usually come through the front also but the deliveries are usually accepted here at the front desk. If the delivery must be made to the apartment, the deliveryman is accompanied by a security guard at all times. Visitors must be approved by the resident and they are logged in and out, with their signatures, any time they visit. As you know there are video cameras here in the lobby and it is taping 24/7. On the night in question, our records show that there were no visitors or deliveries," said the security chief.

"The garage entrance is by overhead door activated by cards issued to every resident. If a card is lost the resident is issued a replacement but only after the lost card's information is deactivated. If someone found a card on the street it would be of no use to them. Residents use the card to activate the overhead garage door for entry. The date, time, and identity of the user are recorded automatically. I guess it would be possible for someone to sneak under the door when opened if the resident wasn't paying attention but they would be stymied once they got in because that same card is required to operate the elevator or the stairwell door lock release. They would not be able to sneak onto an elevator without being noticed," continued the security chief.

"The utility entrance is by key entry through the outside door but to gain entry to the interior of the building the maintenance man must use his assigned card through a single door and his use of the card is recorded also. Our records show only one entry on the day and night in question and that use has been verified as a maintenance call to look at a refrigerator in one of the units but his time in and out was during the morning," said the security chief.

"Have all the records on the night in question been scrutinized and everything verified," asked the FBI agent.

"Everything. And we have only one abnormality during the time frame. At 3:02 AM the records reflect an entry through the garage of one of the residents, a Mrs. Sarah Fleming. I personally interviewed Mrs. Fleming on two occasions and she insists that she was sound asleep at the time. I believe her and have ruled her out as a suspect but the question of the card remains and she insists that her card has never been out of her possession," said the local detective.

"So it boils down to entry by one of two means; through the front entrance with the knowledge and assistance of the security guard or through the garage," said the FBI agent.

"I have ruled out the front entrance entry based on my interviews and the background check on the guard on duty that night which leaves us with the garage entry," said the local detective.

"Even if we conclude that the perp gained entry through the garage, which is the most likely, we have no idea of who he or she is or how they were able to override the system or by some means secure a card," said the FBI agent who was resigned now to chasing dead ends.

"Thank you, gentlemen, for your time," said the FBI agent as he concluded the interview.

G. Lee Greer

Chapter 37

Peck, Vincent, and Mary Leigh arrived in Beaufort for the holidays and were greeted with much joy and celebration. The entire family, including Mary Leigh's mother, Clara Edwards, were on hand and they were obviously in a festive mood. Mary Leigh made every effort to keep her ring finger hidden until they were able to get the announcement made. After handshakes and hugs all around, Peck said, "I have an announcement to make."

Placing his arm around Mary Leigh, Peck continued. "I have asked Mary Leigh to marry me and she has consented."

There was a chorus of applause and pronouncements by everyone, as the news was received enthusiastically. Mother Reynolds and Mrs. Edwards hugged each other and cried with joy. Mary Leigh flashed her ring as she moved around the room to receive the admiration and the congratulations from everyone.

"We are not going to stretch this thing out any longer than is absolutely necessary. We are looking at making it happen within six weeks and we have decided to have the ceremony performed up at the farm. All of you, of course, are invited and we will not accept any excuses for your not being there. It will just be family and a handful of very close friends. Vincent and I will work out all the arrangements to fly everyone up and there is plenty of room for everyone to stay at the farm. We are very excited and we hope that all of you are too," announced Peck.

Mother Reynolds, with her arm around Clara, said, "Peck, Mary Leigh, this has to be the most wonderful Christmas gift anyone has ever received. Clara and I have been conspiring through prayer that this would happen and our prayers have been answered."

The next morning, after breakfast, Peck asked his mother, sister, and brother to meet with him privately to discuss a matter of mutual interest. When they had assembled in the den, Peck said, "I probably should have said something about this sooner but things have been moving pretty fast these last few weeks. I need to advise you of what I have been up to. Since we are each equal owners of the Family Bank, which in turn is the majority owner of Reynolds Commerce, we have equal say in any decision concerning the directions of the companies. It is my recommendation that we sell Reynolds Commerce. I have had some preliminary discussions with some potential buyers and there is every indication that we can sell Commerce at a pretty good premium in today's market. The reason I want to sell is that Mary Leigh and I want to move back home, away from the rat race in New York and Washington. We could hire a management team to run Commerce but it would cost us significant monies to do so and, in my opinion, reduce our asset value in the long haul. Also, we would continue to have oversight responsibility and, quite frankly, I just don't want the responsibility anymore. Mary Leigh and I just want to come home and enjoy each other and our family without the distractions that we would continue to have if we are involved in Commerce."

Mother Reynolds spoke first. "Peck, this is what I have wanted for a long time. You have been away too long. Even if we did not make a dime on Commerce, it would be worth selling just to have you and Mary Leigh at home here in Beaufort."

Sarah and Bill nodded their assent and Sarah said, "Peck, you have done a grand job for all of us and made more money for us than we could ever have imagined but, as Mother says, getting you back home is more important than all the money in the world. We have missed the close association with you all these years and now it is time to reap the benefit from all that effort and that can only be done if you are here with us. You have my vote and my thanks."

Bill added, "Mother and Sarah have said it all. It is just so exciting to know that you will be coming home for good. You do whatever you have to do to make it happen. You do not need to check with us anymore. Just get it done as soon as possible so that we can do some serious fishing and hunting."

Peck looked from one to the other and he saw in their eyes the sincerity in their decision and the love that they held for him. He wept inwardly and wondered to himself why he had stayed away so long from these loving people.

"I will keep things moving along as quickly as I can and keep you posted. Now, let's join the others and do some Christmas stuff," said Peck.

Peck next sought out Vincent and apprised him of the meeting with the family. He was already aware of Peck's intent as he had been involved in some of the preliminary discussions.

"That's great, boss, but we both knew what their response would be. You know, I hadn't considered it before, but I guess that I am going to have to start looking for a new job."

"No, you don't. I am counting on you wanting to move back home too and I have something in mind for you. Besides, I have set aside some of my shares for you so you are going to be a very wealthy man when we sell. You will not have to work at all if you don't want to."

Vincent was visibly moved by Peck's revelation and he had a difficult time responding but finally broke through and said, "Boss, you have done so much for me and my whole family. I could never repay you for all you have done. I too want to come home and get on with my life in a surrounding that feeds my soul and gives it all meaning. This is all so overwhelmingly wonderful."

The holidays sped by with parties, visits and time spent in reacquainting themselves with Beaufort and renewing old friendships. Vincent was seeing Carolyn on an almost a daily basis, much to the delight of everyone. Peck and Mary Leigh spent a couple of days in Charleston with her mother who insisted on showing them around town and seeing everyone she could collar, sharing the news of their upcoming marriage. Mary Leigh was well known and remembered in Charleston and everyone seemed to be thrilled with the idea of them moving back home, even though they would be living in Beaufort and not Charleston. The Charleston folk had a hard time understanding why anyone would not want to live in Charleston, if they had a choice.

Peck and Mary Leigh settled on a wedding date of February 1 and the planning began to work out all the logistics of getting everyone up to the farm for the wedding. They agreed on a guest list which totaled 16 people, most of whom were family. They decided to invite the President and first lady, though they were doubtful they would be able to attend, but they did not want to offend them by not issuing the invitation. Both of them were close friends and admirers of the President.

The holidays came to an end and reluctantly they had to return north. There was a lot to be done by February 1.

G. Lee Greer

Chapter 38

When Peck arrived back in his office he asked his secretary, Helen, to put in a call to the President. Helen came into his office a short time later and advised him that she had spoken with the President's secretary and that the President was tied up for most of the day but that she would get word to him as soon as possible and she felt sure that the President would call him back as soon as he could. Later that morning the call came and Peck answered, "Good morning, Mr. President."

"Good morning, Peck."

"Mr. President, you will be receiving a formal invitation in the next few days but I wanted to call and tell you personally that Mary Leigh Braxton and I are to be wed on February first and we would like to extend to you and the first lady our wishes that you be present if at all possible. We realize that you will probably not be able to attend but we wanted you to know that we would be pleased and honored if you could."

"Peck, this is wonderful news. You and Mary Leigh are two of my favorite people and I am honored that you would want to include Bess and me in your celebration. What time and where is the wedding to be held?" inquired the President.

"The ceremony will be at 11:00 AM down at the farm. It will be a small gathering of just family and some very close friends, less than twenty people." replied Peck.

"Hold on for a minute, will you, Peck?"

In a couple of minutes, the President came back on the phone and said, "Peck, I have looked at my calendar and, with a little reshuffling, it appears that we will be able to be with you. You understand that I have to advise the Secret Service immediately of my plans and they are going to be crawling all over your place from now until the wedding. I hope that it will not be too much of a distraction. Once they have cleared the place they will sort of be in the background and unobtrusive."

"Mr. President, we will be more than glad to put up with the Secret Service just to have you and Bess with us. Just have your people contact me and I will make sure that they get full cooperation. Mary Leigh is going to be thrilled to hear that you and Bess will be joining us. We look forward to seeing you and thank you for wanting to join us and help us celebrate our marriage."

"Goodbye, Peck, unless something unforeseen happens, we will see you there," said the President.

Peck called down to the farm and Mrs. Briggs answered the phone.

"Mrs. Briggs, I am calling to tell you that Mrs. Braxton and I are going to be married and we have decided to have the wedding at the farm. We have set February first as the wedding date and, in addition to family, the President and first lady are going to be there. The total number is going to be about twenty people and they all will be staying there except the President and first lady and another good friend who will be there only for the day. I believe that we have enough rooms to accommodate everyone.

"Mr. Reynolds, that is wonderful news. Mr. Briggs and I could not be happier for the two of you and it is so exciting that you are going to be married here and that the President is coming. I will get started right away and get everything ready. Will you have the reception here also?" inquired Mrs. Briggs.

"Yes, we would like to but we don't want to place too heavy a burden on you. We can easily have the reception catered," said Peck.

There was a momentary silence and then Mrs. Briggs said, "Mr. Reynolds, unless you feel that you need a little fancier menu than I can provide, I would like to take care of the reception myself, with your and Mrs. Braxton's approval, of course."

Peck laughed and said, "We were hoping that you would feel that way and we know that you can outdo any caterer that we could possibly come up with, so we will consider the matter closed. You are in charge."

"Thank you, Mr. Reynolds. I will get started on a suggested menu immediately and it will be ready for your review whenever you wish."

"Tell Mr. Briggs that the Secret Service will be coming down to look us over. He is familiar with their routine since the President has been down before but I will call back as soon as I have talked with them so that we will have some idea of what to expect. Goodbye, Mrs. Briggs."

Peck next put in a call to Mary Leigh. "Hello, sweetheart. Things are moving fast and I wanted to give you an update in addition to hearing your voice."

"Peck, darling, we have only been back for a day and I am already missing you. So tell me what is going on."

"You will be pleased to know that the President and first lady will be in attendance. I talked with him just a short while ago and he seemed genuinely pleased to be invited. I talked with Mrs. Briggs and told her of our plans and she is on cloud nine. I teased her a little bit and suggested that we could have the reception catered if it would be too much trouble for her and when she recovered she let me know in a nice way that she could handle the reception just fine, thank you."

"Peck, you are a devil. I can just see her forlorn face now. I am sure that now that she has thought about it she knows that we would never have considered her not handling the reception."

"Listen, sweetheart, the Secret Service will be calling and I am going to need to run down to the farm for a day or two, possibly this week, and go over everything with them. Do you think that you can sneak away and join me? We can review everything with Mr. and Mrs. Briggs at the same time," said Peck.

"I will be there. Just let me know when. If you can line everything up for Thursday, maybe we can just stay on through Sunday." replied Mary Leigh.

"That's what I love about you. You are so easy and accommodating. I will call you later tonight. I love you."

"I love you, Peck. Goodbye."

G. Lee Greer

Chapter 39

"Sir, I have Mr. Thompson of the Secret Service on line three," Helen informed Peck.

"Hello, Mr. Thompson. I've been expecting your call."

"Hello. Mr. Reynolds. We are going to need to visit with you down at your farm in anticipation of the President's visit. According to our records, the President has been there before, about two years ago, so we will pull our notes and review them and it should save us some time. There is certain information I am going to need from you, specifically, the names and addresses of everyone who will be in attendance as well as any outside persons or concerns that may have reason to come onto the property prior to and during the wedding. I will need complete information on any employees, full and part time, who work for you at the farm."

"I understand, Mr. Thompson. We have been through this exercise before. Mrs. Braxton and I are planning on going down to the farm on Thursday so if you want to bring your people down then, we can get started. In the meantime, I will have my secretary send to you complete information on the guests and the employees. I also have a couple of neighbors who use my barns and pastures and come over daily so I will include them also. If you need to stay overnight you are more than welcome to stay at the house. We have plenty of room."

"Thank you, Mr. Reynolds, but that will not be necessary. There will be a couple of people patrolling the property from now until the President's departure, however, but they will stay out of your way.

"We will be arriving mid to late morning on Thursday. If you get there before us, just see Mr. Briggs, our caretaker, and he will give you any assistance needed," said Peck.

"Thank you, Mr. Reynolds. We will see you on Thursday."

Mr. Briggs picked Peck up at the airstrip around ten o'clock on Thursday morning and advised him that Mrs. Braxton had already arrived and was going over some things with Mrs. Briggs.

"Mr. Briggs, the smartest course for you and me is to stay completely out of the way and just do what we are told," said Peck.

"I learned a long time ago that in matters such as this that is exactly the right thing to do. Even if you think you may have a better idea it is just dumb to offer it unless you are asked. Fortunately, in this case we have two very smart women who know exactly what they want and how to get it done. I think we can rest easy," said Mr. Briggs.

"You're a very wise man, Mr. Briggs," said Peck with a big smile on his face.

Upon arrival at the house they found that Mr. Thompson and his secret service contingent had arrived and they and Peck and Mary Leigh sat down to review how things would play out.

"I know that both of you have gone through this before but I would like to lay it out again so there will be no surprises or misunderstanding. From this point forward there will be a minimum of two of my people on the property 24/7. One will be stationed at the main entrance and the other will be roaming around. All other entrances to the property will be blocked off. No one will be granted access to the property except those persons who have a reason for being here and who have been pre-cleared. A full advance team will arrive three days prior to the President's visit and they will look at everything, and I mean everything, including your personal bedrooms. Any person or vehicle leaving the property will be subject to search upon reentry. We will be installing some extra phone lines which will be removed immediately after things are over. We will try not to disrupt you or your household too much and once we have cleared out, you will not notice that we have ever been here. Now I have a few questions I need for you to answer," said agent Thompson.

"Who will be performing the ceremony?"

Peck looked at Mary Leigh and said, "I hadn't even thought of that."

"Peck, if it is all right with you I would like for my minister to do it. He is currently serving as the Chaplain of the Senate so it should not take too long to clear him." said Mary Leigh.

"That's fine with me."

"Will there be any pre-wedding activities such as a rehearsal or parties that will include any persons not already named by you?"

Again Peck looked at Mary Leigh and she answered, "No."

"Will there be any outside concerns such as florists, or caterers, etc., coming on to the property? If so, I will need their identities."

Peck answered, "There will not be a caterer. Mary Leigh, what about flowers?"

"Mrs. Briggs and I have already discussed this and there will be a floral delivery but it will just be a drop off the afternoon prior to the wedding. She and I will visit a local florist and make the selection."

"That's all I have at the moment. I would ask that you advise your house guests about the security arrangements and ask them to limit their comings and goings as much as possible. The President will be here approximately three hours and while he is here all of our people will be on heightened alert but you shouldn't notice much difference. Everyone should just go about their business and enjoy themselves," offered agent Thompson.

"Mr. Thompson, we hate to put you to all this trouble but the President is a close friend of both of us and we want him to share this important moment with us," said Peck.

"Think nothing of it. This is what we do and as these things go, this should be pretty simple. Now we will get out of your way. Here is my phone number where you can reach me at any time. If any questions come up, give me a call."

After the agents left the room, Mary Leigh said, "Mrs. Briggs has been busy. She has the most wonderful menu for the reception for our approval, would you like to look it over?"

"That's not necessary. If, you are satisfied, that's it."

"I am assuming that you are going to leave all the flower arranging to us also," Mary Leigh said with a grin.

Peck laughed and said, "You already know me too well but if you run into trouble on any particular arrangement, Mr. Briggs and I have already agreed that we will be willing to consult."

"Let's hope that it doesn't come to that."

Mary Leigh continued, "Peck, you know that we are only about three weeks away from the wedding. I am so happy and excited. You know, we haven't even talked about our honeymoon,"

"I have been thinking about that and you just leave that to me. All I will tell you is that we will be away for two weeks and you should pack a tropical wardrobe," said Peck.

Mary Leigh smiled and said, "I know that it will be wonderful. Are there any further developments concerning the sale of Commerce?"

"Things are moving swiftly. We have already agreed on a price, subject to due diligence, which has already begun. If we don't hit any snags we should be able to complete things by April first. As these things go, that is a record speed."

"I called a realtor about selling my house on Monday morning. I gave her a price and on Tuesday morning she brought to me an offer meeting my price. The buyer is from the Middle East and I know him. I guess he plans to use it primarily for entertaining but once he writes the check, that is his business."

"I know that you have a lot to do and will be extremely busy but I hope we can find the time to take a couple of days in a week or so and fly down to Beaufort and start looking around for a place to live," said Peck.

"Just let me know when you want to go. You know, with all the excitement and activity surrounding the wedding in such a short time you would think that I would be pulling my hair out and on the edge of hysteria, but since you asked me to marry you and we decided to move back home, I am completely relaxed and unworried about anything. I have never enjoyed such peace and calmness," said Mary Leigh.

"I know exactly what you mean. I am the same way. Vincent and I were talking last night about this very thing. He too is as calm and happy as can be and cannot wait to get back home to Beaufort. He is also beginning to think very seriously about Carolyn and I could not be more pleased."

"One final thing, Peck. I want us to spend our wedding night down at the cottage."

"And so it shall be," said Peck as he rose from his chair and embraced his love for a long time.

Chapter 40

It was mid January and the politicians were back in town for the reconvened Congress. They quickly reverted to form and the usual backbiting, sniping, and charges were being thrown around. The media were still keying on the conspiracy theory and were beginning to harp on the lack of progress in resolving the case. The Attorney General was bearing the brunt of the criticism and he was looking for answers. He had reconvened the special task force for an update and they were assembled in FBI Director Talbot's office.

"All right, John, let's see where we are," said the Attorney General.

"Sir, we have worked our way through all the cases now, except the Simmons killing, but, as you know, we were in on that one right from the start and I don't know that there's much more we can do there so, in effect, we are finished with our case by case review," responded Talbot.

"And where are we after the review?" inquired the Attorney General.

"Sir, we are right back where we started. We have been unable to come up with anything concrete that would point us in the right direction. We thought that we might have enough circumstantial evidence to proceed with search warrants and more intensive interrogation of Mr. Rollins in the Johnson case but after staff review everyone was convinced that we would get laughed out of the courtroom if we went with what we have, which is basically a lot of suspicion but no evidence," pleaded Talbot.

"People, I was at a cocktail party last night and someone, a senator, asked me how, in this day and age, with all our technology and forensics capability, and with our concentrated effort by a supposedly smart group of people, could eight, very high profile murders go unanswered?" said the Attorney General.

"Sir, with all due respect to the senator, there are literally hundreds of murders that go unsolved every year in this country and these are killings by non-professionals. The people who committed these assassinations were highly trained professionals who know their trade. We have stacks of open, unresolved cases on which we are trying to assist local and state police agencies to solve. Most murders are solved by two means: There is a witness to the crime or the perpetrator does or says something stupid to point to himself. In these cases there is not a single witness and we can count on the perpetrators not doing anything to put them in the spotlight. The reason that there are no witnesses is that our assassins are that good. Now, I'm not trying to start up a fan club for these murderers, but you have to give them their due; they do their work well," interjected Tom Garrison.

"I fully appreciate what you have said, Tom, but, folks, I need something to hang my hat on to deflect all the attention that is the coming our way. How do we do that?" said the Attorney General.

"Sir, one thing you can do is to continue to point out that except in the case of Judge Hammond, these are local jurisdictional matters and that our role is one of assistance to them. We have not accepted these as federal cases simply because there is no legal basis for it. I know that that does not really contribute anything to the solving of these crimes but it just might divert attention from us to the locals," said Jane Henson.

"All right, where do we go from here? asked the Attorney General. We cannot just close up shop and go home and pretend that all this never happened."

"No, we cannot just disband but at the same time we can't keep all these people concentrated on something that is at a stalemate. We would just be spinning our wheels and we have a lot of other things that need attention and resolution. I would suggest that we keep the task force in effect but that we go about our normal business, subject to reassembly if anything significant pops up. In the meantime, I will assign one of my staffers to maintain a desk to receive, coordinate, and disseminate any information that comes up. We will advise the local jurisdictions of the desk and ask them to communicate directly anything of value. I will also have the desk copy Tom in Dallas of any and all new information which may develop. That is my recommendation, sir," said FBI Director Talbot.

"Does anyone here have any other ideas?" the Attorney General asked.

There was no response from any of the others.

"All right, people, we will go with John's recommendation. Thank you for your help. I know that it is just as frustrating for you as it is for me," the Attorney General said as he proceeded around the room shaking everyone's hand.

Leaving the FBI Director's office the Attorney General proceeded to the Whitehouse for a scheduled briefing of the President.

"Good morning, Mr. President," said Attorney General Stevens as he entered the President's office.

"Good morning, Edmund. I hope you are not here to tell me that someone else has been killed by our mystery assassins," said the President.

"No, sir, fortunately everything remains quiet on that front but I did want to tell you where we are and how we are going to proceed, just in case you get questions." replied the Attorney General. He then went on to update the President on the consensus coming out of his just concluded meeting with the task force.

"If you are sure that we have done everything that we can I guess that that is all you can do. I will stress the local jurisdictional angle too if I get questions. If anything pops up, let me know," said the President as he walked the Attorney General to the door.

Chapter 41

On the week of the wedding, Peck, Mary Leigh, and Vincent arrived on Wednesday, as did the full advance team of the Secret Service. The Secret Service went about their business with minimal interruption and disturbance. Peck asked Mary Leigh, Vincent, and the Briggs' to sit down with him to review the logistics of the days ahead.

"The family and Helen, my secretary, will be arriving on Friday. Gil will be flying the family in and Vincent, Mr. Briggs, and I will get them ferried over from the airstrip. We have plenty of bedrooms to accommodate everyone. Mary Leigh and Mrs. Briggs will work out who will be sleeping where. Mrs. Briggs has already planned an impressive dinner for Friday evening. The Secret Service has requested that they be able to place an agent in the floral shop while the floral arrangements are being assembled. Mary Leigh, will you contact the florist and tell them they will be having company and to not start their work until the agent is there? This will save them a lot of time later on. The President and first lady will be arriving at approximately 10:00 AM on Saturday. Bob Stewart, the Director of the CIA and a close personal friend of mine and Mary Leigh's, will arrive at about the same time. So will the minister and Mary Leigh's good friend and her matron of honor, Betsy Winthrop. That will complete the wedding party," said Peck.

Peck continued, "The wedding will be at 11:00 AM with the reception immediately following. Mrs. Briggs and Mary Leigh have the reception well in hand. The President and first lady will be with us until one o'clock. Bob Stewart, Betsy Winthrop and Helen will depart later in the afternoon. That will leave just us and the family here for Saturday evening. Mr. Briggs, who is an accomplished photographer, will be taking pictures at the wedding and the reception. Mr. and Mrs. Briggs have planned a Barbecue for us on Saturday evening which will be down at the barn, so that we won't freeze to death. Mary Leigh and I will spend Saturday night here down at the cottage and we will be flying out late Sunday morning to a destination known only to Vincent, Gil and me. Gil will return here after he drops us off and the family will be flown back home on Monday. Vincent will return to New York after all the loose ends are tied up and then Mr. and Mrs. Briggs will be able to take off their shoes, prop their feet up, and rest for as long as they want."

"Does anyone have any questions or know of anything that I have missed?" asked Peck.

They all looked at each other and Mary Leigh volunteered, "I believe that you have covered everything, Peck."

"Good, now let's enjoy ourselves and in case I forget to say it later on, thank you for helping to make this a wonderful occasion for Mary Leigh and me."

On Thursday Mary Leigh and Mrs. Briggs stayed busy getting the house ready and Peck and Vincent stayed out of the way. On Friday, the family arrived and since they had all been pre-cleared by the Secret Service they entered with no inconvenience.

After hugs and handshakes all around Mother Reynolds said, "Peck, it's so exciting that the President is coming and all this Secret Service attention. Clara and I will have a lot to tell our friends when we get home."

"Well, the President is going to have the pleasure of meeting our families too. He knows how proud we are," said Peck.

"Mr. Briggs will place everyone's luggage in your room and Mrs. Briggs will show everyone where to sleep. After a light lunch, Vincent and I will conduct a brief tour of the place since some of you have never been here before," continued Peck.

"Good. I want to see the horses in particular," said Mrs. Edwards.

"Mother, I hope that you are not going to want to go horseback riding. You haven't ridden in years," said Mary Leigh.

"You never know," said Mrs. Edwards, with a wink.

After lunch and a brief tour of the property, everyone settled in with the elderly ladies taking a nap and the others sitting around enjoying each others company.

"Peck, since your brief visit last week I have found a couple more properties that I think you and Mary Leigh may want to look at. One in particular has just come available and it is a beautiful place; lots of room with about 250 acres, mostly wooded, and a great home in a spectacular setting with about five hundred yards of frontage on St. Helena Sound. If you don't want it, I just may buy it myself," said Bill.

"It sure sounds interesting. Find out as much as you can and Mary Leigh and I will try to get back down there as soon as possible after our return," said Peck.

"How is the sale of Commerce going?" asked Sarah.

"Everything is on track. Unless we run into a snag there's a good possibility that we can close by April first. Vincent will be doing some work on it while Mary Leigh and I are gone and he will probably get some proposal papers, with financial details, down to you to look at," replied Peck.

"By the way, Mary Leigh has already found a buyer for her home and Vincent and I have listed our places with a realtor. In today's market, we shouldn't have too much trouble selling them. Things are moving at a fast pace and before you know it, we will be home in Beaufort pestering all of you," said Peck.

"We can't wait," said Sarah.

On Saturday, the day of the wedding, the President and first lady arrived on time, along with the additional Secret Service contingent. In the front hallway everyone was in a receiving line to greet the President. As the President and first lady exited their car, Peck and Mary Leigh were there to greet them and usher them into the house. Peck and Mary Leigh led them down the receiving line introducing each person.

"Mr. President, I have the honor to introduce to you my mother, Mary Elizabeth Reynolds and Mary Leigh's mother, Clara

Edwards," said Peck as the President and first lady grasped the hands of the two matronly ladies.

"Ladies, it is my honor to meet the persons responsible for Peck and Mary Leigh, two of my favorite people in all the world. I know that you are proud of them and you must be ecstatic about today's event," said the President.

"We are, Mr. President, and we are also pleased to meet you and the first lady. It is so nice of you to be with them on this special day," said an excited Mother Reynolds.

"Mr. President, I am pleased to meet you. You must be all right because my daughter and Peck think an awful lot of you and that means something," said Mrs. Edwards.

"Their friendship and support means a lot to me, both politically, but more importantly, on a personal level. I truly value their friendship," replied the President.

They continued down the line, meeting everyone else and taking the time to chat with each person. The Havel's were in awe of meeting the President and Vincent thought he might have to prop up his mother.

"I understand that you have an interesting story about how you came to know Peck. Maybe later you can tell me about it," said the President.

"Mr. President, it is nice of you to ask about that but you really have no choice in the matter. My mother would have told you that story before you left today as she has told everyone she has ever met," said a teasing Vincent.

"I look forward to it," said the President as he moved on down the line to greet everyone else.

Shortly before 11:00 AM everyone was asked to move into the formal living room where the ceremony would be held. The room was tastefully decorated with fresh cut flower arrangements and seating had been arranged around a trellis arch and kneeling altar. At 11:00 o'clock, Vincent and Betsy took their places and Peck and Mary Leigh entered together to stand before the minister. It took about ten minutes for the ceremony and Peck and Mary Leigh were wed.

At the conclusion of the ceremony, Peck and Mary Leigh turned to receive the well wishes and congratulation of everyone and then they all moved into the adjoining dining room for the reception.

As everyone was enjoying the magnificent spread Mrs. Briggs had prepared, the first lady remarked, "Peck, Mary Leigh, who in the world catered this for you? Everything is absolutely delicious."

"Let me bring the caterer over to meet you and you can compliment her directly," said Peck as he moved away toward the kitchen where Mr. and Mrs. Briggs were busy readying more delicious goodies.

"Mr. and Mrs. Briggs, come with me. Someone wants to meet the person responsible for the delicious food," said Peck as he ushered them towards the dining room.

Peck steered the reluctant couple over to the President and first lady. "Mr. President, your wife wanted to know who prepared the delicious food we are enjoying and I would like to present to you and the first lady Mr. and Mrs. Briggs, the caretakers of this home and, in particular, Mrs. Briggs who prepared the food," said Peck with a smile.

"Mrs. Briggs, we are so happy to meet you and want you to know that we have never enjoyed food more than what you have prepared for us today. Peck, how in the world do you hold on to these people?" asked the first lady.

Mrs. Briggs blushed and said, "Thank you. I'm so glad that you are enjoying everything."

"Mr. and Mrs. Briggs have been looking out for me since the day I bought the property. Everyone who visits here tries to steal them away from me but so far, I have been lucky enough to hold on to them. Even Mary Leigh, before we decided that we could not bear to live without each other, tried to lure them away from me," said Peck.

"I will attest to that," added Mary Leigh.

"Mr. and Mrs. Briggs, it is an honor and a pleasure to meet you. We will not try to lure you away from Peck and Mary Leigh, as they would never forgive us, but we want you to know how impressed we are with what you have done," said the President as he and the first lady grasped their hands.

"Thank you, Mr. President. It is our honor to serve you," said Mrs. Briggs and then they made their way back to the kitchen.

"They will remember this day forever. Thank you for being so kind to them," said Mary Leigh.

As the ladies migrated to and huddled around the first lady, Peck, the President, and Bob Stewart, the Director of the CIA took the opportunity to step out on to the patio with the pretense of enjoying a cigar.

"Peck, Bob, it would seem that our plan has created a new tone in Washington," said the President.

"It does seem so, Mr. President, but we will need to remain vigilant," replied Peck.

Printed in the United States
1245700001B/427-438